GIFT OF FORTUNE

Other books by Ilsa Mayr:

Dance of Life

GIFT OF
FORTUNE

•

Ilsa Mayr

AVALON BOOKS
NEW YORK

For Jamie, again, with gratitude and appreciation.

Chapter One

"What? Would you read that again?" Aileen Bolton asked. "Please," she added, trying to moderate her tone, which had risen to a faint squeak.

The attorney, whose voice had faltered and then stopped, cleared his throat. He started to read the beginning of the document again.

"No, no. Just the last part," she said, fidgeting with impatience.

"All right. 'To my natural son I leave my half of the Triangle B Ranch.' " He stopped and looked at the young woman.

"My father had an illegitimate son?"

"Seems that way."

The attorney glanced at the page again. "His name is Quinton Fernandez."

Aileen shook her head. "That can't be. Are you sure you have the right Jack Bolton?"

Wordlessly the attorney slid the document toward her.

Aileen pried her fingers from the straps of her purse. She picked up the last will and testament. It listed her father's

1

name, address, and birth date. She stared at it for several seconds before she pushed the paper back across the desk. "Mr. Evans, did you know about this . . . this Quinton Fernandez?"

"No. Not until five days ago when Jack's Cheyenne attorney contacted me. I thought about calling you in Washington, but this isn't the sort of thing you spring on a person over the phone."

"Thank you. I appreciate your waiting." Puzzled, she looked at the attorney. "I don't understand why my father hired an outside attorney to draw up his will. Didn't you handle his legal affairs?"

"I did. My guess is he didn't want anyone to know about your half brother."

Aileen jumped up. "He's not my half brother. I'm adopted, remember?"

The attorney blinked. "I'd forgotten that. When Ruth and Jack brought you to the Triangle B, you were . . . what? Two days old?"

Aileen nodded.

"I've always thought of you as their own. Their only child."

"I did too. Until now." Aileen walked to the window and stared out. For a moment she leaned her forehead against the glass pane, which felt cool and soothing. She closed her eyes, trying to focus, trying to come to terms with what she had just learned.

"When? I mean, how old is this Quinton?"

"Twenty-eight."

Aileen stared at the attorney. "He's three years older than I am!" The implication made her reach for the chair and sit. Did her mother know about Quint? What had happened?

"Can I get you something? A glass of water?"

Then another realization hit her. "If he's twenty-eight, then my father," she paused, having a hard time getting the words out. "My father cheated on my mother." Aileen jumped up again. She paced the length of the office. "How could he? My mother was such a fine woman. A real lady. Tender. Gentle. Loving. Generous. Never said a mean thing to anyone or about anyone. Did she suspect? Oh my goodness. She would have been so hurt." Aileen's voice broke. She slumped into the chair again.

The attorney filled a glass of water from the carafe on his desk and handed it to her. "Drink this. Then take a couple of deep breaths."

Aileen took the glass. She pressed it against her left temple, where the first throbs of pain hinted at the beginning of a migraine. She reached for her purse. If she took two pills now, perhaps she could head off a full-blown attack.

"I'm all right," she told the attorney, who was hovering over her. She handed him the empty glass.

"If you're sure—"

"Please go on, Mr. Evans."

"There isn't much more. I can paraphrase it. Bob Williams, the foreman, and his wife, Martha, are given the right to stay rent-free at the ranch for as long as they want. Jack also set up a retirement plan for them. We all knew that. Jack just added it to make it legal and binding."

Aileen nodded. "Good. They're nice people who have been at the ranch for as long as I can remember."

"That's it. And, of course, you keep the half of the ranch your mother left you when she passed away."

"Does this Quinton Fernandez know about his inheritance?" Aileen asked.

"Yes. The Cheyenne attorney contacted him."

"So, my adoptive father knew all along where his illegitimate son was?"

"I don't think so. He asked the other attorney to locate him when he made out this will."

"When was that?"

"A year ago."

"When he learned his cancer had spread." Aileen thought for a moment. "All those years, did he know he had a son?"

The attorney lifted his shoulders in a shrug. "I have no idea."

"Mr. Evans, will you answer a question truthfully?"

"I'll try."

"Did my adoptive father have a reputation for philandering? Did he have other women besides Quinton's mother?"

"Not that I know of. Until I read this will, I'd have sworn that Jack Bolton had led a blameless life. As you know, he was a member of the county commission, the Cattle Breeders' Association, an elder in the church, a—"

"A pillar of the community."

The attorney sighed. "I know the young can be so unforgiving, but try not to be too hard on him. One youthful indiscretion—"

"I know. If there's nothing else, I need to go." Her hand touched her left temple again.

"Shall I have someone drive you to the ranch?"

"No, thanks. I can manage."

When Aileen reached the ranch, she hardly remembered anything of the trip. She had maneuvered the miles on autopilot. She did, however, notice the blue pickup with the horse trailer attached to it parked in front of the barn. Did she have an appointment with a horse buyer? She hoped Bob remembered and took care of it. The afternoon's shocking disclosure had erased everything else from her mind.

Entering the house, she heard the murmur of voices from the kitchen. Not a horse buyer, she decided. Bob would have taken him into the den. Aileen hung her coat in the hall closet before hurrying to the back of the house.

Martha, coffeepot in hand, greeted Aileen.

"Hi, honey. This gentleman has business with you," Martha said, gesturing toward the man who was rising politely from his chair. "And since it's such a cold, drizzly day, I asked him in. You want some coffee? I just made it."

"Yes, I'd love a cup. Thanks." Aileen tossed another glance at the stranger. Her first quick, assessing look had given her an impression of broad shoulders, a slim waist, and dark hair, all handsomely packaged. Her impression had been right. This time their eyes met. His were green, and when his lips curved into a smile, she knew without a doubt that a woman's toes could actually curl inside her shoes.

"I made the coffee good and strong, just the way you like it," Martha said. "It'll warm you up."

"Thanks." Aileen was glad to be distracted from that green-eyed gaze.

"Well, I'll leave you two to discuss business. If you need anything, I'll be in our quarters. Nice to have met you, Quint," Martha said. "Oh, where are my manners? Aileen, this is Quint. I didn't catch your last name, Quint."

"It's Fernandez."

"I better go," Martha said.

Aileen steadied herself by holding onto the back of the nearest chair. To make sure her ears weren't playing tricks on her, she asked, "You're Quinton Fernandez?"

"Yes. And you're Aileen Bolton."

"You didn't waste any time getting here, did you?" Aileen saw his smile fade, saw the jade-green eyes narrow, and felt her face grow warm. She was rarely, if ever, rude, so why now with this man?

"Wrong. I wasted a whole week, waiting for you to get back from your vacation."

"It wasn't a vacation. Two colleagues and I took a group of juniors to Washington, D.C., over spring break. We do this every year so the kids get a better idea about our national government."

"What are you? A teacher?"

"Yes. I teach English at Abraham Lincoln High School."

"Well, what do you know. A schoolmarm."

His voice had assumed a soft drawl. Studying his face and that lazy smile that curved his finely drawn mouth, Aileen couldn't tell for sure if he was being sarcastic, but she refused to be baited.

"I never dreamed that I'd end up with a pretty half sister who's a schoolteacher."

"Your relationship with teachers wasn't that great?" she asked, her voice subtly ironic.

His smile broadened. "That's putting it mildly. But then I never had an English teacher who looked like you."

"Let's get something straight," Aileen said. "We're not related. Jack and Ruth Bolton adopted me when I was a baby." His smile didn't seem to falter, but she had the distinct impression that the warm gleam in his eyes had grown cold. She wondered how much it bothered him that she, an adopted child, had enjoyed the comforts and advantages offered by the Triangle B, while he had been denied them.

"That's too bad. I'd looked forward to having a family."

Slowly his gaze wandered over her in that typical male fashion that Adam had probably used with Eve. Aileen managed to stand without fidgeting.

"Then again, maybe it's better that we're not related,"

he said softly. He picked up his cup and took a sip of coffee.

Put a leather jacket on him, a motorcycle beside him, take ten years off him, and he could be the poster boy for the original teenage rebel without a cause: irreverent, charming, good-looking, wild and ... dangerous. She quickly dismissed the last adjective. She was a grown woman, immune to the charms of the bad boy. She'd come across too many of them in her teaching career to be fascinated by them.

"So, what happens now?" Quint asked.

"Pardon?" Had he somehow guessed where her thoughts had wandered?

"You obviously know about the will. Are you going to contest it?"

"No. That never even occurred to me. If my adoptive father wanted you to have his half of the ranch, so be it."

"If?" he demanded with a raised eyebrow.

"I mean, he obviously wanted you to have it."

"Which half is mine?"

"Pardon?"

"The will said that Jack Bolton's half of the Triangle B was mine. Which half?"

"I don't know. Nobody ever drew a line across the land. I'm sure we aren't supposed to interpret that literally."

"No, I don't suppose so. I'm curious. How did it get to be *his* half to begin with?"

"I'm not sure, but I think it happened when he married my mother. The ranch was hers."

"That explains a lot," Quint murmured.

"Explains what?"

"Nothing." He took a sip of coffee. "The B in Triangle B doesn't stand for Bolton?"

"No. It stands for Bristow, my mother's maiden name."

She watched him nod slightly, as if confirming something in his mind. What was he thinking? Whatever it was, he dismissed it. He fixed her with his intense green-eyed stare.

"So, what do you want to do?" Quint asked.

Aileen blinked. "About what?"

"The ranch. Want to sell it?"

"No! The land's been in my mother's family for over a hundred years." Aileen took a couple of steps toward him, her hands raised as if in supplication. When she realized what she was doing, she dropped them. She squared her shoulders. "This is my home. I'd rather die than leave it."

"You really mean that," he observed. "Do you want to buy my half?"

For a second, joy flooded through her. Then she realized what that meant. Sadly she shook her head. "I can't. I don't have the money."

"Okay. You don't want to sell the ranch or buy my half," Quint said, as if restating her position.

Aileen nodded. "You don't sound disappointed."

"I'm not. Land is a good investment. I just wanted to find out where you stood."

Relief made her knees weak. She sat down. The idea that she would have to leave the ranch hadn't even occurred to her. It should have, and it would have, if she hadn't been so shocked by the will. Aileen drank some coffee. She needed time to think. Also, coffee usually helped her headache, which was showing no signs of going away. She rubbed her temple.

"You have a headache?" Quinton asked.

"Yes."

"Migraine?"

She nodded.

"Ever tried applying pressure?"

"No."

"Here, let me show you." Quint stood behind her chair. Placing two fingers against her left temple, he pressed gently. "I used to do this for my mom when she got migraines."

Aileen closed her eyes. The skin of his fingers felt rough. Obviously he was a man who worked with his hands. What did he do for a living? She'd ask him, but not now. The pressure against her temple felt too good, and magically, the pounding pain dulled.

"Better?" Quint asked, leaning toward her.

He was so close that Aileen felt his breath against her forehead. She merely nodded, as her mouth was suddenly dry. His breath was warm and smelled of coffee. She also caught the faint, cool scent of his aftershave and the familiar smell of leather and horse. It reminded her of her father. She felt the sharp pain of loss, until she remembered that he had kept a stunning secret from her. She could understand his silence while her mother was alive, but why hadn't he confided in her later? That's what hurt the most—his lack of trust.

"Do you get these headaches often?" Quint asked.

"Not really. Mostly they hit me when I'm stressed out." She hadn't meant to admit this.

"My existence stresses you? Well, darlin', I suppose anyone learning that they'd just lost half their inheritance would feel stress."

"Don't call me darlin'. It's condescending," she said, moving away from him. "Thanks for the headache treatment."

"Any time. So, how do you want to arrange this division of property?" Quint asked.

"I thought you didn't want to divide it."

"I don't. Cattle ranching only has a chance of making a

profit if there's enough land. I was thinking in terms of the house."

"The house?" Aileen noticed that her voice had risen again. She sounded like an alarmed mouse. Taking a breath, she asked, "What about the house? I've taken care of it since my mother's death seven years ago. You want to take over?"

"Depends on what kind of housekeeper you are."

She watched Quint run his finger along the top of the cabinets. Aileen stared at him, too stunned to say anything. He was actually checking for dust. The nerve of the man. Clamping her teeth together to keep from calling him a few of the choice words she'd heard her students use, she merely glowered at him.

Looking at the tips of his fingers, Quint said, "Not bad." He opened the refrigerator door and peered inside.

"What are you doing now?" she asked, intrigued in spite of herself.

"Checking to see if you're one of those women who keep only diet food in the fridge." He leaned back to give her a slow once-over. "You don't look like you're obsessed with dieting."

"Are you saying I'm fat?" she demanded.

He grinned at her. "Whoa. I'd never imply that, much less say it to a woman. I don't have a death wish." His gaze lingered on her. "I'd say you're just right. At least for a man who doesn't like squeezing mere skin and bones."

Aileen folded her arms across her chest until she realized that this could be viewed as a protective gesture. Quickly she uncrossed them and picked up her coffee cup. When Quint transferred his scrutinizing gaze to the contents of the refrigerator, she felt relieved.

"Doesn't look too bad," he said after a while. "There's beef, ham, cheese, and a lot of green stuff. But that's okay," he said, his voice magnanimous. "I like a salad with dinner. Are you a fair cook?"

"I can probably match your cooking skills. Unless you've worked as a chef?"

"Nope. Never did, but I've been fixing my own meals for a long time now."

"No wife?"

"No wife, no fiancee, no significant other, as they say. Just a horse." Quint glanced at his watch. "Speaking of horses, I need to feed and stable Sweepstake."

"I'm sure there's room in the barn, but we better check with Bob. He's the foreman. Have you met him?"

"Yes, when I arrived."

"Did you tell him who you are?"

"No. I thought it best if you did that."

"All right. Follow me."

"I know you're not married. I asked the attorney. Are you engaged or seriously involved?" Quint asked as he followed Aileen across the side porch to the small house in which Bob and Martha lived.

For a moment she considered ignoring his question, but he had answered hers. "Neither," she said in a tone that discouraged further inquiries.

"But you have a horse."

"Not really. I teach full-time and keep house. I don't have many chances to gallivant over the range. When I do go for a ride, I use one of the horses from the remuda." Aileen knocked on the door facing them. After hearing Martha's invitation to enter, she opened the door. Bob was sitting in his easy chair, reading the newspaper.

"Good. You're both here, so I won't have to say this twice. You've met Quinton Fernandez. What you don't know is that he's the new half owner of the Triangle B. Jack left him his half of the ranch." Both Martha and Bob stared at Quint and then at her, clearly shocked as well as curious. She'd have to tell them the whole story. "Jack Bolton is, or rather was, Quint's father."

Martha and Bob exchanged a look.

"Quint has a horse that needs to be taken care of. Bob, can you show him where he can stable Sweepstake?"

"Sure thing. This way," Bob said, heading toward the side door.

As soon as the men were gone, Martha followed Aileen back to the kitchen.

"Land's sakes, girl! Isn't this enough to strike a person deaf and dumb? When did you find out about Quint?" Martha asked.

"Mr. Evans told me this afternoon. I didn't expect him to show up so soon, though." Aileen rubbed her temple where she could still feel the imprint of Quint's fingers. Briefly she debated with herself whether she should pump Martha for information or not. Her need to know was too strong to be discreet.

"I asked Mr. Evans this question, but I'm not sure he'd really know the answer, so I'm going to ask you." Aileen faced Martha squarely. "Did my father fool around?"

"Not that I know of." Narrowing her eyes in thought, Martha asked, "How old would you say Quint is?"

"Twenty-eight."

Martha used her fingers to count. Then she nodded. "That fits."

"What fits?"

"About twenty-nine years ago, a group of migrant workers stopped here on their way back from harvesting wheat in Canada. Jack hired them to do some work around the place."

"How come you remember that so clearly?" Aileen asked.

"Because one of the families had a beautiful, young daughter. All the men gawked at her, including Bob. Heck, all men gawk at pretty girls, so I didn't think too much of it when I caught Jack talking to her a few times." She paused, then confessed, her expression sheepish. "I made it my business to know exactly where Bob spent his time, but I should have been more watchful of Jack as well. Not that I could have done anything about him being interested in her."

"So you think Dad was the type to cheat on his wife?"

"Honey, he was a man, wasn't he?"

"You think Mom knew?"

"That's a tough question. If she did, she kept it to herself. She was a lady. She wouldn't have thrown stuff and yelled and hollered."

"Was she happy back then?"

Martha shrugged. "That I don't know. She wasn't one to mope around and complain. I can tell you one thing, though. She sure was happy when she got you. You were the light of her life. There's no question about that. She couldn't have children, the doctors told her, so she convinced Jack to adopt. She once told me that adopting you was the best thing she ever did."

"She was the best mother I could have wished for." Aileen swallowed, willing herself not to allow the unshed tears to reach her eyes. "I hope she was spared knowing about her husband's indiscretion."

"Even if she knew, she wasn't the type who'd give up on a marriage at the first sign of trouble."

Aileen shook her head. "I don't know that I could be that generous and forgiving if a man cheated on me. I'm afraid I'd be tempted to heave every single plate in the house at him and call him every rude name in the book."

A slight noise alerted her to Quint's presence. She hadn't heard him open the door. Uneasily she wondered how much he'd heard of her conversation with Martha.

Chapter Two

"Did you get Sweepstake taken care of?" Aileen asked.

"Yeah. He's in the back stall in the small stable. We thought it best to keep him separated from the other horses till they get used to each other. You have a bunch of great-looking horses out there."

"My d . . . Jack loved horses. After he got sick . . ." Aileen paused briefly, a frown of concentration on her face. "Actually, even before he was diagnosed, he sort of lost interest in cattle. I'd say that for the past two years the only thing that captured and held his attention were horses. Am I right about that, Martha?"

"He always did favor horses," Martha agreed, "but never more so than after he got to feeling poorly. My husband took over the care of the cattle as best he could." She glanced at her watch. "Well, I better get back to my kitchen. Bob likes supper on the table promptly at five-thirty. See you all in the morning."

"Good night, Martha."

Quint wished her a good night too. As soon as the door

closed after her, he turned to Aileen. "Could I have another cup of coffee before dinner? It's been a long day."

Aileen stared at him for a moment. It hadn't occurred to her that he expected to share her meal. She felt like smacking herself on the forehead for being so thoughtless and so dense. She should have invited him. Her social skills were slipping badly. The only excuse she had was that she was still reeling from the events of the afternoon and was, therefore, mentally slow and uncharacteristically disorganized.

"Of course, you may have coffee. Help yourself," she said.

What was she going to fix for dinner? She couldn't remember what she had planned for herself. Opening the refrigerator, she assessed its contents. The ham looked good. But what about side dishes? Both scalloped potatoes and macaroni and cheese from scratch took too long. For herself, she'd slice some vegetables and stir-fry them, but for a healthy young man, that wouldn't be enough. She discovered some sweet potatoes in the vegetable bin. If she nuked them first and then put them in the oven next to the ham, they should both be ready at about the same time.

While Aileen washed her hands, she stole a quick look at Quint. He stood, one slim hip propped against the kitchen counter, studying the wall calendar above the phone on which she kept track of appointments and tasks to be done.

"Looks like you keep busy," he commented.

"Yes. I rarely get home before five, so forget about having dinner at five-thirty. On school days it'll be more like six-thirty or seven before we eat," she warned.

"That's okay." He studied the calendar some more. "What's the A.C. you've written down for every Tuesday?"

"Authors' Club. It's for students who like to write. We

meet after school and critique what we've written," she explained.

"And Y.B. on Thursdays?"

"Yearbook. I'm the sponsor."

"On Monday and Wednesday you've written a-e-r something. I can't make it out."

"Aerobics."

Quint turned around and subjected her to another thorough up-and-down look. Aileen felt herself grow warm all over. She doubted that she would ever get used to those intense, hot-eyed looks that swept over her like laser beams.

"I approve. Everyone needs exercise."

"What do you do?"

"I chase cows, muck out stalls, load sacks of feed, toss bales of hay. Stuff like that."

"So you have worked on a ranch before?"

"Oh, once or twice," he said, his tone dry.

"Since I don't know anything about you, that was not a dumb question," she protested.

"I didn't say it was."

"No, but your tone implied it."

"Don't get huffy."

"I never get huffy."

"Yeah, right."

"Well, I don't."

"Then what do you call it when you lift that straight, aristocratic nose of yours into the air? And toss your hair like that? You're the English teacher. You tell me, darlin'."

Quint called her darlin' to annoy her. She knew that. She wouldn't give him the satisfaction of letting him see her annoyed, even if it meant grinding her teeth down to nubs in the process.

"First of all, I do not toss my hair—"

"Yes, you do. You just aren't aware of it. Reminds me of a spirited little roan filly I once owned. She tossed her mane in the same manner."

Aileen gritted her teeth. When she could speak, she continued calmly, as if he hadn't interrupted her or compared her to a horse. "And second, I am not huffy, or irritable, or testy, or petulant, or any of the other synonyms that come to mind." Like heck she wasn't. The man could irritate the living daylights out of her, and judging by the grin on his face, he knew it. Worse, he enjoyed it. Aileen grabbed the chopping board, placed a zucchini on it, and proceeded to dice it with unnecessary force and speed.

"Easy there," Quint said, moving quickly to stand beside her. "I've tended my share of wounded animals, but I've never tried sewing a finger back on."

"Don't worry. I've done my share of chopping, and I still have all ten fingers. See?" She lifted her hands and wiggled her fingers before she grabbed the board and tossed the vegetables into a saute pan. The oil hissed.

Quint took a step back and blinked. After a couple of seconds he said, "Well, if you're okay, I'll go out to my truck to get some things."

Aileen shot him a long, telling look. "I'm perfectly safe in this kitchen." *Especially with you out of it,* she thought, as she watched him stroll out. He had that insolent, sauntering male strut down pat. And he had a nice back view. Broad shoulders. Narrow hips with just enough curves to fit a pair of jeans perfectly.

Aileen groaned. She had to stop making these inappropriate observations about the man. Like his great back view, or his stunning eyes, or his sexy smile, or his voice which could dip into that low register that was at once caressing and honeyed, teasing and just a little mocking. None of these things mattered. They couldn't matter. Not if they were to work together and make a go of the Triangle B.

Quint paused on the porch. His eyes swept over the outbuildings, the corrals, the range beyond. Half of this was his. He had a home.

Joy welled up in his chest. Looking at the sky, he laughed softly, gratefully, and just a tad triumphantly. For once, fortune had dealt him a winning hand. Then his customary skepticism took over. It hadn't been fate or fortune that had been good to him, but the guilty conscience of a man.

Why couldn't Jack Bolton have had an attack of conscience a heck of a lot sooner? Say fourteen years ago when Quint's mother died? He sure could have used a helping hand then. Water over the dam. Quint shrugged philosophically, dismissing old regrets. Life had taught him not to look back or cry over spilled milk.

With determined steps he walked toward the outbuildings, which, to him, represented the heart of the ranch. Time to look around, assess his inheritance, and decide what needed to be done first.

He checked on Sweepstake. The stallion whinnied at Quint's approach. "Hey, old boy, how are you?" Quint ran his hand under the stallion's thick mane and stroked him. "I think you're going to like it here. Wait till you see the classy, good-looking mares on this ranch. And the classy lady that owns half of it." Quint winked at his horse and left the stable.

Fifteen minutes later he stopped in the middle of the yard, looking thoughtful and slightly puzzled. All around him were signs that indicated the ranch hadn't been taken care of as it should have been. After a long winter, all barbed-wire fences needed mending. He understood that, having spent a good part of his life mending fences in a three-state radius. But on the Triangle B, even the white-painted fences around the house looked like they hadn't seen a fresh coat of paint in recent time.

The barn doors squeaked, needing to be oiled. The gate to the nearest corral was held together with a rope. The tack room was filled with saddles, halters, and ropes needing cleaning, polishing, or some sort of repair. If he'd ever had any illusions that as half owner of the Triangle B he wouldn't have to work hard, they had just gone up in smoke.

What puzzled him most, though, was the absence of a bunk-house. Where did the hands live? A ranch this size couldn't be worked only or even primarily by the owner and the elderly foreman he had met. Looking around, Quint wondered where he would sleep. Briefly he considered the tack room. But it was unheated, and in early March it was still too cold to sleep there. He didn't mind pitching his tent and had often done so, but not when the night temperatures still dipped below freezing.

Shivering, he stared at the house. It certainly appeared to be large enough to have several bedrooms. Convincing that freckle-faced, understatedly sexy schoolmarm that he should occupy one was another matter. Except he owned half the house and had every right to demand a bedroom. He didn't have a choice really, and neither did Aileen.

Making her buy that should be interesting, to say the least. Quint suspected that his teasing banter and line of compliments that usually worked on women wouldn't charm Aileen. She had a way of fixing those lovely blue eyes on a guy that was guaranteed to freeze him in his tracks—if he was a high school student, that is. Since Quint was a decade beyond that stage with the experience to prove it, that schoolmarm trick wouldn't work on him.

With a grin he grabbed his bedroll and his duffel bag and headed for the house.

Inside, he dropped his things in the hall and proceeded to the kitchen. Aileen looked at him from the sink where she was rinsing lettuce.

"Can I help you?" Quint asked.

"Is that a polite offer which you hope I'll turn down?"

"Nope. I'm not into polite offers, so don't expect any. I told you I'm handy in the kitchen. Besides, most of my life I was in a position where, if I wanted to eat, I had to work for it."

"In that case, you can tear the lettuce into bite-sized pieces. Wash your hands first, please."

"Yes, ma'am." He observed her freckled skin turning pink.

"Sorry, that came out like an order rather than a request," Aileen said.

"Must be a professional hazard. As I recall from my school years, teachers sounded more like they were giving orders than making requests."

"Even if I would rather be amiable with students, it's better to be a bit of a drill sergeant. Then they won't try to get away with quite so much," she admitted with a slight smile.

"I'd call that being a little devious."

"And I call it wanting to survive. There's only one of me and a lot of them."

Quint paused to look at her. "You're right. I had never thought of it like that." He dumped the lettuce into the salad bowl. "Anything else you want me to add?"

"Whatever you find in the crisper. There are no tomatoes. This time of year, the ones in the store are so anemic looking and tasteless, not to mention expensive, that I can't bring myself to buy them."

Aileen's reference to something being expensive caught Quint's attention. He watched her face, wondering if she was just frugal or if the ranch was in financial trouble. The signs of neglect could be due to lack of money as easily as to lack of manpower. The Cheyenne attorney hadn't had any information on the financial status of the Triangle B. He would have to find that out from the bank.

Quint watched Aileen move competently between the stove and the table. If she had money trouble, it didn't show, and he knew all the signs of that particular problem. Fascinated, he observed the play of light on her hair. Sometimes it was more red than gold. Idly he wondered what color she called those bright tresses she had tried to tame with combs. He had never found freckled skin appealing— until now. What rotten timing.

For the first time in his life he had a chance to make something of himself, to become respected. He couldn't blow that by becoming involved with this woman. She was his partner. Anything beyond that might interfere with the smooth running of the ranch, might ruin everything. He couldn't risk that.

"What would you like to drink?" Aileen asked. "There's milk, juice, soft drinks, and coffee. After Dad wasn't allowed to drink alcohol, we stopped keeping liquor in the house."

"That's no problem. A glass of milk will be fine."

Aileen filled two glasses and brought them to the table. "We're ready to eat."

They passed the bowls politely and ate quickly.

When they finished, Quint said, "That was a good meal. Thank you. I'll dry if you'll wash. You can tell me where the dishes go. That way I'll get to know where you keep everything. Okay?"

Aileen agreed.

"Some evenings if you're late, I can start dinner. I can't promise to do that often because I notice that quite a few things around here need fixing."

"I know that, but—"

"Hey, don't get defensive. I was just making an observation."

Aileen filled the sink with water. "The man who fixed things around here got married and moved into town. Dad didn't feel up to doing much this past year-and-a-half, and Bob and the hands had more than enough work taking care of the cattle and the horses."

"And you taught school. Did that include summers?"

"No. Those I spent getting my master's degree. There's a considerable jump in salary if you have an advanced degree. It took me three summers, but I finished last August. Hallelujah."

"Congratulations. You prefer teaching to working on the ranch?"

"I don't really know. I was never allowed to work on the ranch. Dad thought that a woman's work was in the house and in the garden." She washed and rinsed the plates before she continued. "I guess it turned out for the best that I went to college and then started to teach."

"Oh yeah? How so?"

"Health insurance. I was able to include Dad on my policy and that saved us when he got sick. The bills were positively ruinous."

Those medical bills might explain some of the neglect on the ranch.

"Last fall I meant to paint the fences around the house, but Dad's illness got a lot worse. He needed more chemo treatments, and I just didn't get around to the chores. Frankly, it didn't seem all that important then."

"Death has a way of putting things in perspective," Quint said.

She looked at him, surprised. Next to the surprise, he fancied he saw a little respect in her eyes. Had she thought he was a complete jerk, too dumb, superficial, or incapable of giving death a second thought?

Aileen broke eye contact. "The plates go on the middle shelf in the last cupboard."

"Okay." By the time the dishes were done, Quint was familiar with the layout of the kitchen. He knew he ought to bring up the question of the sleeping arrangements, but something held him back. The kitchen was warm, peaceful, and homey. A man could get used to this. When he recognized that feeling of longing for a home that crept up on him in unguarded moments, he chastised himself. A man could get soft and careless, and the soft and careless of this world didn't survive. He knew that.

The telephone rang. Saved by the bell.

Aileen picked up the receiver and spoke with someone named Steve. A student? A colleague? A boyfriend? From her tone he surmised that it wasn't a student, but he couldn't decide if it was another teacher or a boyfriend. Whoever the guy was, Aileen seemed to be on good terms with him. Quint didn't entirely like that.

"That was Steve Sanders," Aileen said after she hung up. "He's a history teacher at my school."

"One of your colleagues who went to D.C. with you last week?"

"Yes. How did you know?"

"Something you said about the trip. Do you date him?"

"No. He was involved with someone until recently. We're on several committees together. Lincoln isn't that big a school. You get to know everyone." Dismayed, Aileen wondered why she was explaining this to Quint. It wasn't any of his business whom she dated. "Do you want more coffee?"

"No, thanks." She was changing the subject. Quint wondered if she wanted to date this Steve Sanders, now that the man was available. He watched her pour the coffee down the sink. With her back to him, he couldn't gauge her expression. The overhead light turned her hair into a golden fire.

"Tell me, what do you call the color of your hair?"

Aileen swiveled around to look at him. "Pardon?"

"Your hair. What color do you call it?"

She shrugged. "I don't know. Red-blond, I suppose. Some describe it as strawberry blond. Why?"

"Just wondering." He grinned at her. "I bet you have the same suspicious expression on your face when you're trying to find out if a student is lying about the dog eating his homework."

She couldn't help but smile back at him. "In high school they come up with a lot more sophisticated excuses."

"Like they were changing the oil in their car and it got on the homework, and they didn't bring it because you'd get your hands all gunky? Or there was a burglary at their house and the rotten thief took it?" Quint suggested.

"Those are good, but not for a school in the middle of Wyoming. Here it's more often something like a horse stepping on it, or the wind tearing it out of their eager hands, or their little brother or sister throwing it in the fireplace."

"Not bad," Quint said admiringly.

"I bet you came up with some winning excuses in your day."

He grinned. "I'm not telling."

They finished the dishes.

Aileen dried her hands. She squirted a little hand lotion into her palm and rubbed it into the skin. Then she nudged

Ilsa Mayr

the dispenser toward Quint, who quirked a dark eyebrow at her.

"What? Not a macho thing to do?" she asked.

"When you get to know me better, you'll realize that I never worry about being macho."

"Why? You're that sure of yourself?"

"You got it, darlin'." Quint smiled at her until he saw her expression. "Sorry, I forgot that you don't like being called darlin'," he added.

He wasn't in the least bit sorry, Aileen thought. "I don't mind the endearment in the right situation and with the right person."

"There you go, tossing your hair again."

Aileen opened her mouth to refute his claim but shut it again. She was no longer sure whether this gesture was habitual with her or not. She'd have to ask Jennifer, whom she had known since fifth grade.

She watched Quint rub lotion into his hands.

When he caught her glance, he said, "It feels good, and I like all things that feel good."

"A hedonist, huh?"

"If that means I appreciate pleasure, then I am a devout hedonist," he said, his voice suddenly soft.

Was he flirting with her? Aileen risked a quick glance at his handsome face. When she met his green-eyed gaze, she knew what the phrase "smiling eyes" meant. He was definitely teasing her, maybe even flirting with her. Quint was undoubtedly better at this flirting thing that she was. She felt heat rise into her face again, knew her pulse was beating faster, while he seemed calm. Drat. She took a deep breath.

"I have to grade some papers," Aileen finally said, her voice faint.

Clearly she was waiting for him to leave. The time had come. "Well, if you show me to my bedroom, I'll retire and leave you to your grading."

Quint watched her reaction closely. She stood as if turned into a pillar of salt. Her eyes widened in shock. Then she shook her head slightly, as if she couldn't believe what she had heard. Aileen started to speak, but her voice failed her. She swallowed visibly.

"What did you just say?" she managed to ask.

"I said, I needed a place to sleep. I didn't see a bunk-house. I double-checked all the buildings."

"We don't have a bunkhouse anymore. It burned down about five years ago. We didn't rebuild it. The hands live in trailers down the road."

"Is there an empty trailer?"

Aileen shook her head.

"Well, it's too cold to pitch my tent. And I'm too old to sleep in the barn. That was okay when I was fourteen and fifteen, but not now." He hitched his left shoulder, feeling the slight ache that had plagued him since he took a hard spill off the back of that rodeo bull.

"How about a motel?" she asked.

"I've stayed in a motel while waiting for you to return from your trip. That gets expensive fast. Maybe you can afford it, but I can't." Still she didn't say anything. She wasn't making this easy for him.

Quint walked to the hall and glanced around. Turning back to face her, he said, "Judging by the downstairs, this house must have three or four bedrooms." He saw the color drain from her face.

"You want to sleep in this house?" Aileen asked and reached for the table to steady herself.

"Seems the logical and practical thing to do."

"You can't! This is my house. My home," she cried out.

"Wrong. This is *our* house. *Our* home. Remember?"

Aileen's knees grew weak. She sank into the nearest kitchen chair.

Chapter Three

Aileen didn't know how long it took for the room to stop swaying. She was holding onto the edge of the kitchen table for dear life.

"Look, I'm sorry I sprang this on you so bluntly," Quint said, "but I thought it had to have occurred to you that I needed a place to sleep."

"Well, it hadn't! Until a few hours ago I didn't even know that you existed, much less that you'd be invading my home. And needing a place to sleep." Aileen pressed her hand against her temple.

"Darlin', if my sleeping in the same house is what's bothering you, it shouldn't. I like tall, pale blondes or tiny, fiery brunettes. You're neither, so you're safe from me."

Aileen knew her mouth dropped open but she couldn't help it. The man's arrogant assumptions were as astonishing as they were disturbing and insufferable. And then he had the audacity to level one of his killer smiles at her. Gathering her dignity around her and lifting her chin, she said, "It's reassuring to know that I'm not your type, and since *you* are not *my* type either, you'll be perfectly safe

29

from me as well." She thought she saw his smile falter for a second.

"Now that we got it settled that we're not going to tear each other's clothes off, I'd like to turn in. I've had a long day. Where do I sleep?"

That was a good question. There was no way she could give him one of the upstairs bedrooms. The idea of his sleeping down the hall from her was just too. . . . Aileen couldn't think what it was that disturbed her so about it, and she didn't have the time to figure it out. Ruling out the upstairs, that left the first floor.

"If you don't mind a room that's not completely redecorated, you can have the small parlor. There's a bathroom across the hall from it."

"I'm not fussy."

"That's good, because this house has no maid service. I'll do most of the cooking, but you do your own personal laundry. The washer and dryer are in the utility room, which is next to the kitchen."

"That's acceptable," Quint said.

That was big of him, she groused silently. "The ironing board is in there too."

"Ironing board?" he asked, puzzled.

"Don't you iron your shirts?"

"No. I have my dress shirts done, and the work shirts? The cattle don't care if they're ironed or not."

"You have a point," Aileen conceded. "Just to clarify things," she added, "You can use any room on the first floor, but the upstairs is mine."

Quint lifted an eyebrow, but then inclined his head in agreement.

"Follow me." Aileen led the way. She opened the door and turned on the light. "Oh. I'd forgotten that we had left the stepladder and the worktable in here." Aileen picked up the ladder.

"Here, let me." Quint wrested the ladder from her. "Where do you want it?"

"Just put it in the hall."

When he returned, she said, "Jennifer, she's my best friend, and I were putting up new wallpaper. Her baby came down with a cold, and then I had to go to D.C., so we didn't have a chance to finish. I'll call her and ask if she can help me this weekend. I can't hang wallpaper by myself."

"No hurry," Quint said. He pulled the dustcover from a piece of furniture. A loveseat. Did Aileen think he could sleep on this midget couch?

She lifted the dust sheet from a single bed next to the window. "I'll get a pillow and some sheets."

He watched her leave. She was quick and graceful. Probably had taken dancing lessons as a girl. And studied the piano, and . . . Quint dismissed these thoughts. It wasn't her fault she had enjoyed privileges. She'd been lucky, and he hadn't. That was life.

Quint sat on the bed to test the mattress. Not too soft. A man could get a good night's rest in this bed. With a sigh of relief, he pulled his boots off.

When Aileen returned, she handed him a thick, fluffy pillow. "Can you put the pillowcase on it?"

"Sure." The pillowcase had yellow stripes woven into the white fabric. The yellow matched the sheet Aileen tucked over the mattress. The cover of the comforter she spread over the bed matched the pillow. "I can't remember if I ever slept in such a color-coordinated bed."

Was there a mocking undertone in his voice? His face gave her no clue. "You don't like it? My mother didn't like plain linens. She said that if you could have glorious color, why settle for white. I'm pretty sure we don't have any white sheets. Maybe Martha has—"

"This is fine," he reassured her. "It looks pretty and inviting. I'm sure I'll sleep just fine in this bed. Relax, Aileen."

Relax? He had to be joking. She might never relax again. She straightened the edge of the comforter one more time. "If you don't need anything else, I'll say good night."

"What time do you get up in the morning?"

"Six. Earlier if I don't get all the papers graded."

"In that case, I'll start the coffee. And I'll make it good and strong. Just the way you like it," he said, repeating Martha's words.

"Thanks."

"Good night," Quint said.

Aileen hurried into the kitchen. She put the teakettle on. If ever she needed a calming cup of herb tea, it was now. She retrieved her briefcase from the hall and stacked the spelling work sheets on the table.

Ordinarily, she graded papers wearing her comfortable robe and fuzzy slippers, but with Quint in the house, that didn't seem such a good idea. Briefly she debated running upstairs to change into jeans and a T-shirt and get out of the pantyhose she'd been wearing all day, but that would only waste time.

She poured a cup of tea and picked up the first sheet. Would Quint be warm enough with just the comforter? The nights still got awfully cold.

Aileen went to the linen closet for a blanket. She paused in front of his closed door to take a deep breath. She knocked. When he opened it, she forgot momentarily what she was going to say. He had taken his shirt off. Mutely she stared at his wide shoulders and broad chest. That glorious expanse of skin and muscle seemed to be all her eyes could look at.

"Yes?" Quint asked.

"Um. I brought you a blanket. I remembered that the heat register is closed in this room. You should open it. The nights are still cold."

"Thanks. I will."

Then, remembering why she had knocked on his door, Aileen thrust the blanket at his chest. "Here, you'll need this." When he took the blanket, his fingers brushed against her hand. She jerked back as if scalded and, for the second time that evening, covered the short distance to the kitchen in record time. This could become a habit—her hasty retreat to the relative safety of the kitchen.

Aileen sat down. She sipped some tea. Then she picked up the top sheet. She blinked when she read the first word. What on earth was *gerrenty?* Then she remembered that *guarantee* was a word in the short story her freshmen class was reading. With a sigh she picked up her red pen. She had a feeling she'd be using it a lot.

She had graded about half the quizzes when she heard the shower start. Oh, great. Now she had a naked man taking a shower in her house. Noting the absurdity of her thought, she shook her head. Of course Quint was naked. People didn't take showers with their clothes on.

Unbidden, the image of his bare chest flashed into her consciousness. She pictured water sluicing over his handsome face, over his strong shoulders, down his chest, matting the fine, dark hair.

"That does it," she muttered. "I'm going upstairs."

The first thing Quint became aware of the next morning was the seductive aroma of coffee. Aileen must not have finished grading those papers last night. He glanced at his watch. Five-thirty. He had overslept, but that was not surprising. He hadn't slept well the whole week while waiting for her to get back to the ranch.

When he had finished getting ready, he joined her. "I see you're still at it," he said, nodding toward the stack of papers.

"Sometimes it's easier to face these atrociously spelled words in the morning." Aileen hoped Quint would buy her explanation. "How did you sleep?"

"Like a baby."

Lucky him. It had taken her hours to fall asleep, and then her sleep had been plagued by bizarre dreams in which he and his sexy smile had played a leading role.

"Looks like the coffee is ready. Want me to pour you a cup?" he asked.

"Yes, please."

Quint studied the mugs hanging from a rack. With a grin he picked the one with a big, red apple on it. He read the inscription. "From a fan?"

"Last year's senior class. I was their advisor. It's customary to say stuff like that about the class advisor."

Quint doubted that, but let it pass. He filled the mug and handed it to her. Then he filled one for himself. Sipping the fragrant brew, he studied Aileen. Her hair hung in shiny reddish-golden waves to below her shoulders. She looked very pretty and very young in her quilted satin robe that she had buttoned all the way to her chin. He wouldn't have thought that pink was a good color for fair skin and caramel-colored freckles, but this particular shade looked great on her.

"What are you going to do today?" she asked.

"Look around. Meet the hands. Decide what's to be done first."

"Will you consult Bob? He's been the foreman for as long as I can remember."

"It would be dumb and shortsighted of me not to consult him."

She nodded, relieved.

"Did you think I'd throw my weight around? Give high-handed orders? Maybe fire someone?"

"I hoped you wouldn't, but since I don't know you—"

"You didn't know what to expect."

"Exactly."

"Aileen, I may not be as educated as you, but I'm not stupid."

"I didn't say, or even imply, that you were."

"My . . . what is the buzzword? People skills? They're good." They'd had to be for him to survive. "I *can* run this ranch, Aileen."

"Again, I didn't say that you couldn't. And for both our sakes, I sure hope you can."

"For the last year-and-a-half, I was the foreman on a ranch in the western part of the state." Quint took a business card from his wallet and handed it to her. "You can call Mr. Vance and ask him for a reference. I—" A knock on the back door stopped him.

"Come in," Aileen said.

"Mornin', folks," Bob said. "Martha's fixin' a big breakfast. She hopes you can join us."

"I have to finish grading these papers, so I can't, but Quint, why don't you go? You can talk about the ranch while enjoying Martha's excellent cooking."

"Sounds good. Thanks for the invitation, Bob."

"Martha was takin' the biscuits out of the oven, so why don't we go. She gets cranky when her food gets cold."

"See you tonight," Quint said to Aileen.

She watched the men leave the room, glad to be alone.

She had been acutely aware of Quint's silent study of her and had almost regretted her small act of defiance—if coming down to her kitchen wearing her robe rather than her school clothes could be called an act of defiance.

A knock on the door interrupted her thoughts. She didn't even have a chance to say "enter" before Martha swept in, carrying a plate.

"I brought you a couple of biscuits and some blackberry preserves that you can eat while reading your papers."

"Thanks."

"Quint sure got here early."

"He never left," Aileen said.

"What do you mean, he never left?"

"He slept here."

Martha's jaw dropped open. She perched on the nearest chair and leaned toward Aileen. "Say that again."

"Quint spent the night here."

"Saints above protect us from the demons below," Martha murmured. "Why?"

"Because we don't have a bunkhouse, and he had nowhere else to go."

"How about a motel?"

"For one thing, the nearest motel is over forty miles away, and for another, neither of us could afford to pay for a motel night after night."

"But he can't stay here," Martha said emphatically.

"Why not? Half this house belongs to him. Remember?" Aileen straightened the stack of papers and slid them into her briefcase. "Martha, I said Quint spent the night in this house. I didn't say he spent it in my bed."

Martha gasped. Her hand flew to her mouth. "Mercy, girl. I never suspected he did. Miss Ruth raised you better than that."

"Then what's the problem?"

"The problem is that we don't know nothin' about him. The man could be a swindler or a convict or worse."

"The lawyers checked him out thoroughly to be certain that he's not a swindler or an impostor. And if he had a criminal record, they would have discovered that as well and told me."

"But you're both young and unmarried. It just isn't proper. And Quint's so good-looking." Martha's voice had risen into a wail.

"If Quint were ugly, would that make it less improper?" Aileen asked, her eyebrow raised.

"Oh, you know what I mean. People are going to talk! And you're a schoolteacher."

"Martha, we're now in the twenty-first century. Surely two people sharing a large house they both own isn't going to cause a major scandal."

"Maybe not in a big city, but here? I wouldn't be too sure. You be careful," Martha warned.

Martha twisted her wedding ring, a sign, Aileen knew, that she was uneasy. "What's the matter?"

Martha shrugged. "Oh, all right. Which room did you give Quint?"

"The small parlor."

"Downstairs? That's good."

"I'm glad you approve," Aileen said, her voice dry. "I hope you remember that this is an old house and that all the doors are sturdy and can be locked."

Martha looked a little sheepish. Then she rose. "I better go see how the men are doing. Eat your biscuits."

"I will. Thanks, Martha."

Jennifer arrived on Saturday morning, ready to work.

"Where's the baby?" Aileen asked, after greeting her friend.

"My mother-in-law is babysitting her so I can stay until after lunch."

"Great. We should be able to finish wallpapering the room."

They had cut and hung the second panel when Jennifer sucked in her breath in that audible manner that indicated surprise. "What's this?" she asked, holding up a pair of boots. "And this?" she demanded, picking up a shirt from the love seat.

"That's a flannel shirt," Aileen said.

"No duh, but it's a *man's* flannel shirt, and don't tell me it belonged to your dad, because he never wore anything this brightly colored."

"No, it wasn't Dad's shirt."

"Aileen, you got a man living in this room, don't you?"

"Yes."

Jennifer dropped the boots.

Aileen had never seen her friend so stunned. It took a good five seconds before Jennifer found her voice.

"Man, if the saying 'still waters run deep' weren't so old, I'd swear it was coined especially for you. I can't believe this. You were always so . . . so straight-laced and proper."

"I'm not straight-laced," Aileen protested. "Careful and choosy. Maybe."

Jennifer collapsed onto the love seat, still clutching the shirt. "Who is he?" she demanded.

"His name is Quinton Fernandez and this isn't what you seem to think it is." Aileen then proceeded to tell the story as succinctly as she could.

"Holy—." Jennifer clapped her hand over her mouth. Now that she was a mother, she was trying to clean up her language. "Holy horseradish! Your dad? Of all men, I'd never have suspected him of having a baby on the side.

Just goes to show that you can never tell about people."
Jennifer shook her head. "And this Quinton really owns
half of everything? Is that legal?"

"He does, and it is."

"What's he like?"

Aileen shrugged.

"Aileen! This is no time to clam up. What does he look
like?"

"He looks okay."

"He looks okay? What does that mean? Is he plain? Is
he ugly? Is he cute?"

"Your husband is cute. Quint is more . . . adventurous-
looking. Now come on and help me with this panel. We
have to get this done. You'll meet him at lunch."

"If I'm not dead of curiosity by then," she muttered.

Despite Jennifer's difficulty in concentrating on the task,
they got the room wallpapered by 11:30.

Jennifer, hands on hips, looked at their work. "I must
say this room looks great. I wasn't so sure about this green
textured wallpaper when I first saw it, but it works in here.
You always had good taste."

"Thanks. I need to check on lunch," Aileen replied.

"I'll clean up in here."

Ten minutes later the women had set the table. Jennifer
was pouring the third glass of milk when Quint walked into
the kitchen. Staring at him, Jennifer kept pouring, even
though the glass was full. Fortunately, she was doing this
over the sink. Aileen dashed to her side and rescued the
carton of milk.

While returning the milk to the refrigerator, Aileen made
introductions. Judging by Quint's smooth, gracious response, he must have encountered Jennifer's slack-jawed,
undisguised admiration more than a few times before.
When she met his green-eyed gaze, Aileen knew he was a

little amused as well, but since it was a good-natured amusement, she decided to overlook it. Jennifer had been her friend since fifth grade. She could not allow anyone to be maliciously amused at her friend's expense.

They concentrated on eating for a while. At least, Quint and Aileen did, while Jennifer, with a stunned look on her face, stirred her soup.

"This is great soup," Quint said. Peering closely, he analyzed the contents. "Lots of vegetables, chunks of tender beef and . . . rice?"

"Barley," Aileen said.

"I suspect this soup didn't come out of a can," Quint said.

"Not in this house. Miss Ruth made everything from scratch and she taught Aileen to do the same," Jennifer said. "My mom, on the other hand, couldn't put a meal together if you took away her cans and boxes. Aileen's been giving me cooking lessons. Andy loves it."

"Andy is Jennifer's husband," Aileen explained. "Help yourself to more soup."

Quint refilled his bowl and took another sandwich. "Do you live near here, Jennifer?"

"I live in town now, but I grew up on a ranch just south of the Triangle B. My folks still live there."

"Must be nice to have lived in one place most of your life," Quint said, his voice musing.

"Or boring. Where did you grow up?" Jennifer asked.

"All over." Quint shrugged. Then, focusing on Jennifer, he asked if she had children.

Aileen noticed that Quint had deftly changed the subject from his past to Jennifer's baby. Why was he so reluctant to talk about himself?

When they had finished dessert, Quint rose. "Thanks for lunch, Aileen. I'm working on the north range, mending fences, so I'll be back late. I can fix myself something when I get back. Nice meeting you, Jennifer."

"Nice meeting you too." Jennifer waited until she heard the back door close before she spoke. "*Okay*-looking?" she said, her tone incredulous.

"What?"

"You said he was *okay*-looking. Do you need glasses? Quint's positively yummy. He's hot, hot, hot. Even a happily married woman like me sees that." Jennifer used her hand to fan herself.

"Looks aren't everything."

"No, but they sure don't hurt. Did you notice he was sort of evasive about where he grew up?"

"I noticed."

"What *do* you know about him?"

"Not much. He works such long hours that we haven't had a chance to talk. He comes in to eat dinner and then he goes out again, working in the tack room or the barns. He certainly is a hard worker; I'll give him that. And Bob says Quint seems to know a lot about ranching. I hope so. I'd sure hate to lose the Triangle B."

"You always did love this place. Me, I couldn't get into town fast enough." Jennifer paused. "He isn't married, is he?"

"Who? Quint?"

"Of course, Quint. Who else are we talking about?"

"He said he wasn't. Or engaged or involved. He told me that right off the bat."

"Interesting," Jennifer mused.

"Why?"

"Did he ask if you were involved?"

"Yes."

"Even more interesting." Before Aileen could ask why, Jennifer said, "He was testing the water."

Aileen rolled her eyes. "We have to get along to hang onto the ranch, so it's better if we keep this strictly business. Ranching hasn't been all that profitable lately. The Triangle B will require all of our attention."

"Or you could get married and make this a doubly solid partnership."

"Like that wouldn't present another set of problems? Besides, I seriously doubt that Quint's the marrying type."

"Any man's the marrying type if he has a strong incentive or if he meets the right woman," Jennifer claimed with conviction. "Now I better go and retrieve my baby. Andy's mom wants to go shopping."

As Aileen walked Jennifer to the door, Jennifer asked, "Do you have any plans for tonight? It's Saturday, you know."

"I have papers to grade and bread to bake."

"You're going to wait up for him, aren't you? And have something hot waiting for him?" When Jennifer saw Aileen's expression, she added quickly, "Hot to eat, I mean. A man who works that hard deserves a hot meal at the end of the day."

"Good-bye, Jennifer. Thanks for the help."

Even though her friend was obviously matchmaking, she was right about a man deserving a hot meal. Aileen decided to cook something that would keep warm in the oven.

By the time Quint got back to the ranch, it had been dark for several hours. He hadn't meant to stay out that late, but fixing the fence had taken longer than anticipated. He was dead tired, cold, and hungry.

The house was quiet. Aileen had gone to bed, or, more likely, she was out on a date. This was Saturday night, after all. He felt acutely let down that she wasn't there. When he identified the source of his disappointment, he called himself a fool. The woman was nothing to him. She could be nothing to him.

Something smelled temptingly good in the kitchen. A note on the counter informed him that food was in the oven and a salad was in the refrigerator. Aileen sure was big on salads. He filled his plate from the casserole and carried it to the kitchen table. He had almost wolfed it all down when Aileen joined him.

"I thought you were out," he said.

"No, I was upstairs. Reading." She fetched the salad and the dressing and set both in front of him. Then she placed the casserole on a trivet and brought it to the table. "You may as well finish this. It doesn't keep well. The noodles become soggy."

He didn't need urging and scraped the last bit of chicken, noodles, and vegetables onto his plate. He also dutifully ate the salad.

Aileen carried the casserole to the sink and washed it. "What were you doing out there so long?"

"Mending the fence."

"In the dark?"

"Kept the headlights of the truck aimed at the fence. I wanted to finish that section. No sense in wasting time driving all the way out there again tomorrow."

"Tomorrow is Sunday. Everyone has the day off." Aileen put the casserole into the cupboard before joining him at the table. "Quint, you don't have to kill yourself with work. No one expects that."

"What did you expect? The south-of-the-border guy with the sombrero pulled over his eyes taking a nap in the noon-day sun?"

"That's a terrible ethnic stereotype," she said, her voice and expression shocked. "I didn't have time to form any expectations. You were here before the surprise of your existence wore off. I wasn't able to speculate about you or form any preconceived ideas."

Quint carried his dishes to the sink. He turned the radio on and moved the dial until he found a station playing music.

"How come you're not out on a date?" he asked. "It's Saturday night."

"I got out of the habit of dating, I guess. Dad was sick for so long. When he was home, he needed care. When he was in the hospital, I visited him every evening. And since his death. . . ." her voice trailed off. Then she realized that his voice, his expression held a challenge. Squaring her shoulders, she asked, "What about you? You were out repairing the fence instead of kicking up your heels in town."

"True. Let's fix that," Quint said, and approached her.

What does he have in mind, Aileen wondered, her heart thudding.

Taking her hands, he pulled her to her feet. "Let's dance."

"Dance? I'm not a good dancer."

Putting his arms around her, he said, "Don't worry. I am."

"Why does that not surprise me?" she murmured. "You do everything well that involves women, don't you?"

"Are you accusing me of being a gigolo, or are you asking for a demonstration?"

He smiled at her lazily. His green eyes sparkled. Aileen felt her breath catch. "Neither, but—"

"If you don't want a demonstration, hush up and dance. You think too much."

"I don't believe that's possible."

"Yes, it is," he insisted. "Sometimes you have to listen to your instincts. Feel instead of think."

"That could be dangerous."

"Your life could stand a little danger."

His words, his voice, soft and husky, sent a shiver down her spine. She ought to pull out of his arms and run upstairs and lock her door. But she didn't. She would wait until the music stopped. After all, she didn't want him to think that he was dangerous to her. He wasn't.

The music changed to a slow beat. Immediately his arms tightened around her and he drew her close.

Aileen smelled the fresh, clean, cold air of the range clinging to him. She felt the hard muscles of his arms, felt the intimate warmth of his breath against her temple, and could no longer lie to herself. This man *was* dangerous to her.

Chapter Four

T he week passed so quickly that Quint didn't realize it was Friday night until Aileen dumped the thick folder of weekly compositions on the kitchen counter. She brought a huge stack home each weekend to be graded.

Early Saturday morning he was scheduled to participate in a rodeo. He was tempted to cancel, but since he had already paid the entry fee, he felt obligated to go. He could also use the money he was confident of winning in at least two of the events. Quint didn't tell Aileen where he was going or what he was doing in the note he left for her on the kitchen table.

He knew Aileen was asleep the moment he returned late Saturday night, for the house had that muted feel to it that it assumed once the echoes of human voices and movements had been absorbed by the walls. Quint knew that silence well, having crept regularly out of windows of the many foster homes of his teenage years to roam the night, seeking something, anything, to calm the rage hammering inside his skull.

When Quint entered the kitchen on Sunday morning, he

knew immediately that Aileen was upset with him. Although she answered his greeting in a quiet, polite voice, the rigid stance of her body signaled unapproachability. He poured himself a cup of coffee.

She was all dressed up, wearing a belted, long-sleeved dress the color of pine needles and high-heeled brown pumps. She had tamed her bright hair into a complicated knot that rested against her slender, elegant neck. It was the sort of knot a man's hands itched to undo. Did women fix their hair deliberately like that, knowing it drove men crazy?

"Going somewhere or coming back?" he asked, watching her over the rim of his cup.

"Coming back. I went to early service." She turned the page of a spiral-bound notebook.

"Grading?" he asked.

"No. Planning the menu for the coming week."

"You're a very organized woman."

"Is that a criticism?" she asked, looking at him for the first time since he had come into the kitchen.

Quint noticed that she was trying to keep her expression disinterested and indifferent, but he thought he detected hurt lurking in the blue depths of her eyes. He had some fence-mending to do, and it wasn't just the fences out on the range.

"Being organized is good," he said, "provided you leave a little room for spontaneous action."

"Such as?"

Quint shrugged. "Watching a sunset. Listening to the song of a bird. Smelling the new grass on a spring morning. Taking in a movie on the spur of the moment. Going dancing. Stuff like that."

"Or stuff like going off for the weekend without telling anyone where you could be reached?"

"Ah. So that's what's bothering you," Quint said. "I thought it might be." Involuntarily, he rubbed his aching shoulder.

"What's the matter? You got hurt? Or is it a hangover?"

"I got thrown."

Thrown on his rump over a woman, Aileen suspected. Out loud she asked, "In a barroom brawl?"

Anger flared in him, but he beat it down. "Why is it women always assume the worst about me?"

"Do they? I'm sure you'd know the reason for that better than I."

Quint set his cup down forcefully. Had it been fragile porcelain, it might have cracked. He took her arm and forced Aileen to face him.

"Look at me, and let's get this out in the open."

"You don't owe me an explanation," she claimed quickly, trying to sound convincing.

"The heck I don't."

"No, really—"

"Aileen, be truthful. Don't pretend indifference. You know as well as I do that if I don't explain, the atmosphere in this house will be cold enough to hang a side of beef."

Aileen opened her mouth and snapped it shut. Somewhat shamefaced she said, "I'm just used to everyone on this ranch telling if they're going to leave, where they're going, and when they'll be back. Last year this saved the lives of a couple of men during a snowstorm. Of course, if you had a hot date for the weekend—"

"My date was with a cantankerous bull that didn't want to be ridden and some ornery calves that didn't like being roped."

Aileen blinked, sorting through this information. "You went to a rodeo? I mean, you took part in it?"

"You sound as shocked as if I'd told you I robbed the bank in town."

"Why wouldn't I be shocked? What if you'd broken your arm, or your leg, or——"

"I didn't. And this was my last rodeo appearance. I only went because I'd already paid the entry fee. No sense in forfeiting it. And it was a way to earn some quick cash."

Aileen stared at him. Though Quint was good at reading women, he wasn't quite sure how to interpret her expression. She was different. Educated. Classy. Not the sort of woman who hung around rodeos or frequented honky-tonk bars. Not the sort of woman he usually met. Her steady blue-eyed stare unnerved him a little. "What?" he finally demanded.

"Quick, easy cash? Is that what you're after?" she asked. "Is that what you want from life?"

The unspoken criticism in her words sliced into his pride. Wounded, he said, "First of all, there's nothing *easy* about earning money rodeoing. And second, by quick I meant extra. Additional. If you don't already know it, what ranch hands earn doesn't rank on top of the pay scale."

Aileen blushed. "I'm sorry. I didn't mean to imply that rodeoing is easy. I know a number of men who've been hurt, including Jennifer's dad. He's been a semi-invalid since a bull gored him. It made life for the family very hard. I know rodeo work is dangerous. I think it's quite. . . ." She broke off, unwilling to finish the sentence.

"It's what?" Quint asked, his voice challenging.

"You really want to know?"

"Spit it out."

"I think it's stupid. Why ride an animal that was never meant to be ridden? Why risk being crippled or killed? This makes no sense to me." She paused to study his face. Defensively she added, "You wanted to know what I thought."

"I did. I suppose most women feel the same way. Except the groupies. They—" Quint swallowed the rest of what he'd almost blurted out, realizing by the widening of Aileen's eyes that mentioning the groupies had been a mistake.

Aileen folded her arms across her chest. She pictured sexy young things wearing tight jeans and push-up bras hanging on his arms, gazing at him adoringly. She didn't particularly like the image. "Groupies? Of course. Every male activity that has some glamour to it, even if it's shoddy, will have a female following. And I bet they were all over you."

Quint shrugged, his expression as sober as he could manage. It was obvious that Aileen didn't like the idea of groupies surrounding him. That pleased him. "I never encouraged them," he claimed.

He wouldn't have to, she realized. This irritated her. He wouldn't have to do a single thing and women would follow him, and the more disinterested he acted, the more persistently they would try to catch his attention. They probably unbuttoned their blouses, swished and swayed their hips, and paraded shamelessly in front of him to get him to notice them.

"But I bet you didn't *discourage* them," she said, her voice cold.

Quint grinned. "When I was eighteen, nineteen, I naturally thought life couldn't get any better than having women chase me. What red-blooded young buck wouldn't think that?"

"And when you got to be twenty-seven, twenty-eight?"

He shrugged. "I still like women. I'm pretty sure I always will, so sue me."

Aileen leveled a long look at him.

Quickly he added, "But groupies no longer interest me."

"Yeah, right.

"Really. It's the truth."

"Why not? Seems to me you wouldn't have to woo them, or wine and dine them to charm them into your bed." Aileen saw his jaw clench and his eyes narrow and knew she had crossed a line.

"Are you saying a rodeo bum isn't supposed to be choosy? Have any standards? Is that what you're claiming?"

"No. I'm sorry if I implied that. I didn't mean it. And I didn't call you a rodeo bum."

"You're too well brought up to say that out loud, but I bet you thought it."

"I wasn't thinking that. Until a few minutes ago, I didn't even know you followed the rodeo circuit."

"I never followed it full-time. I only entered events that were near the spreads where I worked."

"To earn extra money."

"Primarily, but I won't deny that it wasn't also thrilling. To a kid who'd been in and out of a half-dozen foster homes and agencies, who'd been considered wild and incorrigible, a little applause, a little recognition, was like salve on an open saddle sore. We didn't all grow up where you were given gold stars or words of praise and validation."

Aileen looked at him for a long moment. "I can't even begin to imagine what your teenage years were like."

"Darlin', you don't need to imagine my youth. I don't need your pity," he snapped.

She had hurt his feelings again without meaning to. With a pang she realized that behind that handsome, reckless facade, he hid barely healed wounds and an easily hurt pride. She would have to be more careful with her words.

"Looking at you, I'd never presume to offer you pity," she said. "I'm sure men envy you and women adore you."

"Horses and dogs like me too," Quint said, his tone self-mocking.

"I don't doubt that. You could probably charm the proverbial birds out of a tree as well," she said, matching his ironic tone. Then growing serious, she said, "What I meant was, I feel compassion for the boy who had no home."

"Well, the boy's all grown up, so save your compassion."

So much pain beneath that fierce pride. Aileen wanted to touch him, to . . . What? He didn't want compassion, and anything else was inappropriate. The tone of his voice told her that the discussion of his past was closed. At least for now. Aileen knew she wouldn't be able to leave it alone. She was always interested in people, so how could she not be intensely curious about Quint? She had never known a man like him.

She glanced at him. He hadn't shaved this morning. The dark stubble reinforced the aura of quiet danger that clung to him. Men would hesitate to tangle with him and women, if they had any sense of self-preservation, would cross the street when they saw him coming. And here she was, sharing a house with him. Heaven help her. The pressure around her lungs increased as if she had dived too deeply into the gray-green water of an unknown river.

"Have you had breakfast?" Quint asked.

"Only coffee."

"Why don't I cook us some flapjacks?"

Visualizing chewy, bland pancakes, she said, "Why don't we cooperate in fixing breakfast? There's a loaf of bread that's beginning to go stale. It'll be just right for French toast."

"Sounds good to me. What do you want me to do?"

"Set the table and pour juice. But first, get me two eggs from the fridge and the milk."

"Yes, ma'am."

Aileen ignored his mock-serious tone of voice. She cut the loaf of homemade bread into thick slices. Then she beat the eggs with milk, added spices, and soaked the bread in the fragrant liquid.

Quint sniffed. Whatever it was Aileen had added to the milk reminded him of her scent. He didn't know if the fragrance was due to perfume or was the natural smell of her skin; he hadn't been close enough to her to determine that. In any event, the scent made him think of the caramel on top of the flan his Aunt Ramona used to make. She wasn't really is aunt, but a kind woman who had taken him in after his mother's death. Unfortunately, a stroke had lamed her and sent him to his first foster home.

Dismissing thoughts of the past, he completed his tasks. Then he brooded over their earlier conversation about easy money and values as he watched her saute sausage patties in one pan and French toast in another. His initial assessment had been correct. He would have to prove himself to her, and that wouldn't be easy. She had high standards. Then and there he resolved that he would not only meet her standards, but surpass them. He would show her that he was good enough for her.

While they ate, Aileen turned the conversation back to the rodeo. "It's not that I disapprove of the rodeo as much as I simply don't understand it. What would possess a supposedly sane man to climb on the back of a bull who's been raised to be snake mean and chronically ill-tempered?"

Quint thought for a moment before answering her question. "I suppose the same thing that makes men climb snow-capped mountains, or race cars at death-defying speeds, or surf killer waves. The challenge. The danger. The satisfaction of doing it and surviving. The competition."

Aileen shook her head, signaling that this was incomprehensible to her. "You said this was your last rodeo competition?"

"Yes." Quint waited a beat. "Do you believe me?"

"I would like to, because the alternative is more than a little scary. What if you got hurt and were laid up for weeks, or months? Bob is past retirement age. He stayed on only because Dad got ill. He promised to work until I hired a competent foreman, but that could take time. I could learn to run the ranch, but that would take time as well. In the meantime, we could lose half the cattle and subsequently the land." Aileen paused to take a breath.

"I'm aware of what's at stake. I told you, I only entered because I'd already paid the fee. And the money I earned will cover my personal needs for quite a while."

"Why didn't you ask—"

"No! I've never asked a woman for money, and I'm not about to start now," Quint said, his voice rock-hard, his eyes emerald bright.

Aileen felt heat cover her face. "I'm sorry. We should have talked about money sooner. My fault. I was so caught up in all that's happened that I didn't think clearly."

"No need to apologize."

"Yes, there is," she insisted. He had risked his life riding a wild bull because she hadn't faced facts. "Let's talk about it now," she said. "This is how we've managed the finances in the past. I use part of my salary to buy groceries and pay the utility bills. Dad has . . . had an account for his personal expenses and an accountant who pays the hands and whatever the ranch needs. You should have an account too. And if this arrangement meets with your approval, we can continue it."

"I already opened an account." Quint paused, trying to frame his words carefully. "Do you have any idea what kind of financial shape the ranch is in?"

"No. Dad refused to discuss such things with me."

"I'm only asking because we need to make some long-term financial plans if the ranch is going to make a profit. Don't you agree?"

"Yes. I think we better take a trip to the accountant's office."

Quint nodded. "When can you go there with me?"

Aileen studied the wall calendar. "Not until Friday afternoon, but I'd like to know before then what shape we're in. If I call Mr. Holloway and tell him about you, are you willing to go there by yourself?"

"Sure. Why not."

"I'll phone him from school tomorrow."

It turned out that Mr. Holloway had retired. He'd kept the Triangle B as a client only as a favor to its late owner. The accountant had left for a monthlong vacation in Florida. His secretary assured Aileen that the hands had received next month's salary, that the feed bill had been taken care of, and the taxes had been paid. More than that the secretary couldn't tell Aileen, but she promised to have the accountant get in touch as soon as he returned.

When she told Quint that evening, he nodded thoughtfully. "At least we know everything's taken care of for the next month. After that, we'll see."

"I can't believe that the ranch is in serious financial trouble," Aileen said. "I mean, wouldn't Dad have said something?"

"Would he? Did he confide in you about ranch problems?"

Aileen shook her head, chagrined. This had always been a sore point, and for Quint to realize this so quickly was embarrassing. "In some ways he was a dinosaur. As I mentioned before, he claimed a woman's work was limited to the house and the garden. My mother was the only exception to this."

"Did he confide in your mother?"

"He must have. She kept the books. He hired the accountant after she died." Aileen pushed a piece of meat around on her plate, her appetite suddenly gone. "Of course, my mother kept the books before she got married. After her father died, she was in charge of the ranch for about five years. She knew everything about it and managed it successfully until she got married."

"When you were growing up, did you think you were well off?" Quint asked.

Aileen considered this question at length before she spoke. "Yes. We took vacations. We had nice clothes. In addition to the pickup, my parents each had a car which they always traded in for newer models long before the cars needed to be replaced. I had a college fund which paid for tuition." She shrugged. "We weren't poor. At least I don't think we were."

Quint chuckled, but it was a cynical sound rather than a humorous one. "I'm an authority on being poor, so let me assure you that you definitely weren't."

She studied his face, trying to gauge how much it had hurt him to have gone without when she'd had everything. His expression was unreadable. If anything, he looked tired. And he was also worried about something. "Quint, what's wrong?"

"Nothing, probably."

Aileen put her fork down. She carried her plate to the sink, where she set it down with unnecessary force. Then she whirled around to face him, her expression mutinous and determined. "Don't you dare do this to me. It's bad enough your father put me off with evasive answers. I had to take it from him, but I don't have to take it from you."

Quint covered the distance between them with deceptive speed. "Don't call him my father. Ever."

The anger in his green eyes caused Aileen to want to move back from him, but he had her trapped against the counter. She raised her chin. "Jack Bolton is your father. Or rather, *was* your father, whether you like it or not. Maybe he wasn't a great father—"

"*Maybe* he wasn't a great father? That lousy excuse for a man. . . ." Quint forced the rest of his words to stick in his throat. He balled his hands into fists. He took a painful breath. "Let me tell you about the man you call my father. Jack Bolton saw a lovely, innocent young girl, filled her head with false promises, and seduced her."

Aileen felt the blood drain from her face. "What promises?"

"What do you think? That he would marry her. Leave his wife. What else? The miserable liar."

"No!" Aileen placed her hands over her ears.

"You asked. Now you have to listen." Gently Quint pulled her hands from her ears. "When she got pregnant, he discarded her like a worn-out saddle."

Aileen shook her head vigorously. "Discarded her? That's not possible. Maybe she left because her folks were leaving. Are you sure he knew about you?"

"Oh, yes, he knew. When my mother wrote him, telling him again that she was pregnant, he denied being responsible. He sent her a couple of hundred bucks hush money and told her never to bother him again. If she or any member of her family ever set foot on the Triangle B, he'd sic the dogs on them."

Aileen gasped and swayed as if he had struck her. She clutched the edge of the counter behind her to steady herself. "I can't believe he could have done that," she cried out in protest.

"Why not? Because he was good to you and your mother?" Quint looked into her eyes, which were dark blue pools of shock, anger, and misery. He knew it was cruel to tell her this, but she had asked. "Aileen, you said the ranch belonged to your mother's family. Think about it. According to Bob, Jack Bolton blew onto this ranch like a tumbleweed, owning nothing more than a beat-up pickup, good looks, charm, and an overwhelming determination to improve his station in life."

"Just like you," she snapped, and immediately gasped, appalled at her own words. But she was too angry to apologize.

"True," Quint said, his voice harsh. "Except I was invited. Or summoned. I didn't manipulate a woman into giving me half ownership of this ranch." She looked as if she might faint. Realizing that Jack Bolton might have taken advantage of her beloved adoptive mother was obviously painful to Aileen. She turned away from him. Her head dropped forward, exposing the soft, vulnerable curve of her neck. Without conscious thought, Quint laid his hand on her neck, a gesture meant to be comforting.

"I'm sorry. I shouldn't have said this. Maybe Jack did love your mother. Maybe he was only heartless to mine." Quint turned her to face him. She was so pale that the caramel-colored freckles on her face stood out in stark contrast.

"I don't know what to think," she whispered. "I'd like to believe that he loved my mother." Aileen took a shuddering breath. "Still, your story is proof that he was capable of cruelty, deceit, and irresponsibility."

Aileen's voice sounded strangled, as if it were being squeezed out past unshed, bitter tears. Quint stroked her hair.

"Did my fa . . . did Jack ever send money to help support you?"

"No. Never." Watching her grow even paler, he said, "Aileen, let it go."

She couldn't let it go. She had to know. "Did he know where you were?"

"My mom wrote him when she took sick."

"Did he respond?"

"He returned the letter with a fifty-dollar bill and wrote not to bother him again."

"Oh my God," Aileen murmured. She stifled a sob, though she could not stop the tears that ran down her face.

Quint's fingers traced the curve of her neck. "Don't cry, for heaven's sake. None of this is your fault. Besides, all this happened years ago. It's almost forgotten."

"As if something like this could ever be forgotten," she cried out.

"Maybe not forgotten, but you learn to live with it."

A violent shudder shook her body. "I can't believe this. My mom used to say not to mind him when he was super critical or aloof. She said it wasn't his way to show affection. Now I wonder if she was wrong about him—if he ever cared about anybody but himself."

"Surely he treated her and you well." Quint didn't add that it was in Jack's best interest to treat his wife decently. "He didn't mistreat either of you, I'm sure."

"No, he was polite and solicitous. Most of the time he called her 'Miss Ruth,' which I always thought was quaint and sweet, but now I wonder if this was just another way of keeping an emotional distance."

"How did he treat you?" Quint asked.

"Mostly he ignored me. Mom said he was too busy to pay much attention to us, so I tried hard to make him notice me."

"How?" Quint asked.

"By getting good grades and doing everything that was expected of me."

"Did it work?"

"Minimally. I've often wondered if he might have paid more attention to me if I'd messed up and gotten into trouble."

"Maybe. Out of curiosity, why didn't you?"

"I couldn't do that to my mother." Aileen bit her lip, trying to control her trembling voice. "In retrospect, I realize that most likely he agreed to my adoption only because it meant so much to my mother. And probably because he felt guilty for cheating on her." A new burst of tears followed that admission.

Quint placed his arms firmly around Aileen and held her. The murmuring, soothing sounds of his voice slowly calmed her sobs. With his face pressed against her neck, he inhaled her scent. He hadn't been mistaken. Her skin smelled a little like caramel, making him long for that sweet, melted-sugar taste of all the feast days of his childhood.

He moved his head lower until his lips touched her neck. He meant to kiss her neck just once, but that wasn't enough. She was so delicious that the taste, the touch, the scent of her fogged his ability to think. With a small groan he pressed a series of kisses on her skin until he felt her tremble. That stopped him cold. What was he doing? Had he lost his mind? Had he forgotten that to him, kissing the tender neck of a woman was a potent aphrodisiac that nearly broke his control?

He released her abruptly. "Sorry, Aileen," Quint murmured, his voice husky, and fled from the kitchen.

Aileen stared after him as if in a trance. Her senses, her mind, her body were all in a turmoil. She felt as if the world as she had known it had disappeared. Her father, who had merely seemed cool and distant, had been unmasked as a selfish, cold, cruel, immoral man. Could Quint possibly be wrong? He had seemed so sure, had told his story so convincingly.

And then Quint had held her and comforted her. She thought he may even have kissed her neck. Why? What was that all about? She felt so confused, ungrounded, cut off at the knees. A sob escaped from her burning throat. Then a new torrent of tears nearly blinded her.

Holding onto the kitchen counter, she made her way to the pantry. There, shielded in its near darkness, she sank to the floor. She hugged her knees to her chest. Surrounded by the familiar, homey smells of strings of dried peppers, sacks of beans and onions, bottles of sweet clover honey, and tins of cinnamon and ginger, she allowed herself the luxury of weeping tears she had repressed since her mother's death.

Chapter Five

Quint left the house before Aileen got up the next morning, for which she was unspeakably grateful. She wasn't sure she could have faced him with even a minuscule measure of equanimity.

Raised in a house where raw emotions were always held in genteel control, the memory of her tearful outbursts in front of Quint was unsettling—as was her subsequent weeping in the pantry. Aileen couldn't remember ever letting go of her feelings like that before.

In the bright light of morning, she was certain that Quint had kissed her neck. And not just once. Several times. Soft kisses whose power had flashed like hot light to the very ends of her extremities, even as she was reeling from shock. How was that possible? He had destroyed the image of her father she had carried in her heart, had smashed the past as she had known it, while at the same time making her aware that she was a woman and he a man. This was insane.

Aileen groaned in dismay. Maybe Quint was mistaken. Maybe he didn't know the whole truth about what had happened between his mother and Jack. Maybe . . . Aileen shook her head. Quint was living proof that Jack Bolton had cheated on his wife. Had fathered a son for whom he had taken no responsibility. There was no denying that Quint was her adoptive father's son. Even if Jack had not acknowledged him, the resemblance was too strong to ignore. True, Quint's hair and skin were darker, but his features bore a striking resemblance to Jack. And then there were those unmistakable, brilliant green eyes. How many people had eyes like that?

Aileen pressed her fists against her temples. It seemed that since Quint's arrival, she was perpetually hovering on the edge of getting a migraine. A migraine she could handle, but how on earth was she going to deal with last night's disclosures?

She brooded about this for long minutes. No matter how disappointing, how disillusioning, how bitter, she would have to learn to live with the new image of her father. Grit her teeth and accept it. What about the other? About Quint holding her? Murmuring comforting sounds and kissing her neck? The longer Aileen thought about it, the more she convinced herself that a few kisses on her neck were nothing to get unhinged about. Maybe if it had been a long, passionate kiss on the lips, she might have something to worry about. Such a kiss would undoubtedly indicate a physical attraction on Quint's part, but kisses on the neck were more . . . comforting? Yes, he had only meant to comfort a weeping woman.

Somewhat reassured, Aileen bathed her eyes repeatedly in cold water until the puffiness induced by her marathon crying jag was reduced. She planned to visit her friend and mentor, Dora, on her way to school. Aileen dressed carefully, knowing that even though her mentor was ill, her instincts were as sharp as ever. Dora Callahan could detect

the slightest variation in mood and emotion with one glance
from her perceptive eyes.

In the kitchen, Aileen cut the coconut cake she had baked
in half and placed one portion in a bakery box. Then she
put two blueberry muffins in a bag and filled a basket with
meal-sized portions of chicken, ham, and beef. If her mentor would allow it, Aileen would gladly fix all her dinners,
but Dora was a proud woman, fiercely clinging to her conviction that she could take care of herself.

Aileen left a half hour early. She caught a glimpse of
Quint and the hands as she left the ranch, but didn't think
he had seen her. She was relieved, for she didn't know if
she should have waved, nodded her head, or what. She
hated feeling unsure of herself.

Quint heard Aileen's car start. Though he was listening
intently to Bob's comments about the south range, he was
sharply aware of her car moving down the driveway. When
she didn't stop, he felt the tension ease from his stiff shoulders.

He knew the reprieve was only temporary, and that he
would have to face her in the evening. Maybe by then he
would know what to say, how to explain his unexplainable
behavior of the night before. Just now he had no idea why
he had kissed her.

That was not entirely true. He had kissed Aileen because
she was crying, because she needed to be held, because she
smelled so sweet, because she had a lovely, elegant neck
that begged to be kissed—and because he had succumbed
to impulse.

Every single one of the many caseworkers and counsel-
ors who had supervised his long trek through foster homes
and the child welfare system had urged him to fight his
risk-taking impulses, to think before he acted, and to con-

sider the consequences. After some hard knocks and disappointments, he had finally seen the wisdom of their advice. He tried hard to curb his impulses, and usually he succeeded. Last night he had not.

Why had he failed? Aileen wasn't his type. Quint ruminated over this all the way to the south range. Even though he had told Aileen that he preferred blonds and brunettes, that wasn't strictly true. Physical appearance had never, or rarely ever, been the deciding factor in choosing his female companions. Rather, it was the women's willingness to keep the relationship lighthearted, with no promises, with no expectations of anything more than mutual pleasure and fun.

He strongly suspected—no, he knew—that Aileen wouldn't be interested in that kind of relationship, but increasingly, he wasn't either. Now he wanted more.

The problem was that logic told him that the only relationship he ought to have with Aileen was a business partnership. No messy emotions. No long kisses. The thought startled him. Why did he think she would be passionate? On the surface, Aileen was lady-like almost to the point of uptightness, and he sensed strongly that she was somewhat inexperienced. Yet something about her suggested hidden fires, barely acknowledged hungers, and slumbering passions.

Quint's throat suddenly felt dry. He had to stop speculating about Aileen. That was none of his business. It couldn't be. Folk wisdom said that nothing ended a friendship faster than lending or borrowing money. From his own observations he had learned that nothing ended any kind of business partnership faster than emotional involvement. Telling himself to remember that, he turned his attention to the south range.

* * *

They had eaten their muffins and enjoyed the Earl Grey tea, made small talk about school events, the weather, and how soon the tulips might bloom when Dora, without missing a beat, said, "Now tell me, Aileen. What's really on your mind."

"Why do you—"

"The truth, please. I'm recovering from quadruple bypass surgery and can't waste my strength on evasions and equivocations. What's going on?" Dora refilled their cups and then leaned back in her chair with an expectant expression on her face.

Aileen took a deep breath and told Dora about the will and Quint. Her mentor listened attentively, but Aileen could tell that even the unflappable Dora was stunned. She downed her tea as if to gain strength, or time, or both, before she spoke.

"This story contains all the ingredients of a Greek tragedy, or a Restoration comedy, or an afternoon soap opera, depending on how you look at it," Dora said.

Agitated, Aileen cried out, "This is not a story. This is my life!"

"I'm sorry, dear. I know this isn't a story. It's just that it is so hard to believe that Jack Bolton . . ." Dora's voice trailed off. She stared into space. Then she nodded. "On second thought, it isn't so unbelievable. Remembering his hands, I'm not surprised to learn that Jack had a streak of ruthlessness in him."

"I don't understand. What about his hands?"

"They were almost square. See how our four fingers are of unequal length? How there's roughly a half-inch difference in length between them?" Dora held up her hand to illustrate. "The three middle fingers on Jack's hands were almost the same length. And his fingers were broad, blunt, brutal-looking. If I had been here the summer your mother married him, I would have tried very hard to keep her from doing so. She was my friend, the younger sister I never had."

Although Aileen was used to her mentor's odd beliefs, which she had acquired from a lifelong study of history and world cultures and their more bizarre facts, this time Dora seemed to have gone too far. "On the basis of Jack's hands you would have advised my mother against marrying him?"

"You sound shocked, but physiological manifestations of a person are most often a good indication of character. But in this case, I had other reasons."

"Such as?"

"They don't matter anymore," Dora said. "Both Jack and Ruth are dead." Dora refilled her cup. Then she added, "Your grandmother opposed the marriage. She never liked Jack. Never thought he was good enough for her daughter. And she let Jack know exactly how she felt about him. Those first years of their marriage while she was alive and living at the ranch with them couldn't have been easy for him."

Aileen sipped her tea, thinking. After a lengthy silence she spoke. "You were my mother's best friend. Do you think she knew about Jack cheating on her with Quint's mother?"

"Yes. Ruth never said anything specific, but I'm quite sure she knew."

"Oh, gosh. How awful for her," Aileen whispered.

"I'm sure it was devastating at first, but in some ways it made the marriage stronger. Jack stopped running around and became a serious rancher."

"He ran around?" Aileen whispered, stunned.

"What I meant was, he'd drive to the roadhouses on the

highway. I'm not sure he necessarily did anything more than have a few beers, play poker, and shoot pool."

"What caused him to reform?" Aileen asked.

"Guilt, probably, and Ruth gave him—" Dora stopped abruptly and busied herself refilling their cups.

"What?" Aileen asked.

"I've already said too much."

"No. You've come this far; go on. I'd like to know the truth," Aileen urged her.

"The truth about relationships is often overrated and disillusioning."

What could her mother have given Jack Bolton that changed him? Or seemingly changed him. Then it hit Aileen. She felt the blood rush to her face. "Ruth gave him half the ranch, didn't she?" From Dora's expression, she knew she had guessed right. "She bought him with thousands of acres of land."

"That's a little harsh, don't you think? The man worked the land. Giving him half the ranch probably made him feel less like an outsider. And Ruth loved him."

"And love makes everything right?" Aileen demanded.

"No. Love has nothing to do with something being right. It's a powerful force that isn't subject to reason or logic or even ethics. It's a law unto itself." Dora studied Aileen. "You obviously have not been in love."

"Have you?" Aileen asked forcefully. She regretted the impertinent question as soon as the words left her mouth. "I'm sorry. I had no right to ask that."

"It's all right. Just because I'm a spinster doesn't mean I never loved a man."

Aileen looked at Dora speculatively. During the school year her mentor led the quintessential spinster's life—living alone in her little house with only her cat for company, her garden as a hobby, her charitable works to fill the winter months.

Yet every summer she traveled. What she did during those worldwide odysseys, as she called them, nobody knew. She could have had wild flings all over the globe, or a longtime married lover with whom she spent the halcyon days of summer. More and more Aileen was convinced that it was impossible to know anyone completely.

"How about you? Are you seriously dating anyone? Steve Sanders, now that he broke up with his girlfriend?" Dora asked.

"Why does everyone assume that?" Aileen demanded.

"Maybe based on the way Steve looks at you when he thinks nobody's watching?"

Aileen stared at her mentor. "I never noticed him doing that."

"You wouldn't. Are you interested in him?"

"No!"

"That was a strong, unhesitating answer," Dora said, pleased.

Aileen herself was surprised by the emphatic no she had uttered. Even as recently as spring break she would have gone out with Steve. What had changed? Then it hit her: Quint. Aileen's heart skipped a beat. No sooner did that green-eyed cowboy move into her house and she was ready to dismiss one of the most sought-after bachelors in the county. What was wrong with her?

"I was afraid you might be interested in Steve."

"Afraid? Why afraid? What's wrong with Steve? There's hardly a single woman around who doesn't give him a second look."

"No doubt. He is nice-looking, and has that boyish charm that attracts a lot of women, but have you studied his mouth? The way it often droops?"

*First a man's hands and now another's mouth. Was
Dora losing it?* A quick glance at her mentor showed her
to be alert and bright-eyed.

"No, I can't say that I've noticed Steve's mouth." But
Aileen was quite sure that if Dora had handed her a piece
of paper and a pencil, she would have been able to sketch
an accurate image of Quint's mouth. This was not good.

"Well, I have yet to meet a man whose lips have that
downward slant who wasn't given to fits of petulance and
whining," Dora said with authority. "And those are not appealing qualities in a man. Or in a woman."

"No, they are not," Aileen agreed. What would Dora say
about Quint? He didn't have a droopy mouth, and his
hands, though strong and rough from work, were not brutal-
looking.

"Tell me about Quint," Dora requested.

"He doesn't look anything like Steve."

Dora leaned forward. "Does he have those sexy, dark,
smoldering Latino looks?"

"His eyes are green. Like his father's." Aileen wasn't
ready to talk about Quint. She took a last sip of tea and
rose. "I must go or I'll be late for homeroom. Call me if
you need anything." Aileen rushed from the room, but not
quick enough to miss Dora's final question.

"When are you going to bring Quint to meet me?"

Aileen stopped in her tracks. She knew she couldn't keep
him a secret forever. It was amazing that not more people
had found out about him already.

"I'll bring him soon," she promised.

Quint curried Sweepstake until the stallion's coat
gleamed. Then he looked around the stable, but there was
nothing else for him to do. He could no longer put off going
to the house.

Hunching his shoulders against the rain, he sprinted across the yard. He didn't see Aileen's briefcase and purse in their usual place and felt relieved. She wasn't home yet. Quint wasn't sure, though, whether he was more relieved or disappointed. At least he had time to clean up. After a quick shower and a change of clothes, he hurried to the kitchen.

Aileen arrived just as he was adjusting the seasoning of the chili. "Here, taste this and tell me what you think." Quint dipped a spoon into the chili and handed it to Aileen. "Careful, it's hot." He would hate to see her sweet mouth get burned. He watched her blow on the chili.

"How is it? Too spicy?"

"I like spicy. It's good." She licked the spoon. "Actually, it's very good."

"Or maybe you're just hungry."

"Both," she admitted with a smile. "It's been a long day and our aerobics instructor really worked us hard." Aileen took her raincoat off. Though Quint hadn't said anything, she sensed he was dying to do so. "What?"

"Men should erect a monument to the guy who invented spandex."

"How do you know it wasn't a woman?" she demanded.

"Let me restate this. Men should erect a monument to whoever invented spandex."

Aileen pretended to be indifferent to his implied compliment, but inwardly she was smiling. "Do I have time to look through the mail before we eat?"

"You have until the noodles are cooked. We're having chili mac. You want chopped onions and cheese on top of yours?"

"Neither, thanks, but I will cut up carrots and celery so we have something crunchy on the side."

Quint grinned at her. "I wondered if you'd fix a salad."

Aileen raised an eyebrow. "When you live to a healthy, ripe old age with all your teeth in your mouth and all your hair on your head, you will thank me."

His grin widened.

"What?"

"You tossed your hair again. But I like it," he added hastily. And that was the problem. He liked the gesture too much. It made him want to reach out and stroke those silken tresses. Curl his fingers around them. Lift them off her delicate neck and. . . . *Don't even go there,* he warned himself. Some men went crazy over legs; some got turned on by bosoms. With him it was a lovely neck that made his blood hum.

Quint lifted the lid and stirred the noodles. Fortunately, Aileen was busy cutting carrots into sticks. She couldn't have sensed his hot preoccupation with her hair and her neck. Then he frowned. Something in her comment had finally registered with him.

"Am I in danger of losing my hair and my teeth? Did my . . . did Jack Bolton lose his?"

"No, but my mother always served a balanced meal."

"Mine was glad when she could put enough tortillas and beans on the table." Though he had his back to her, he sensed her shocked expression. "I didn't mind. I thought everybody ate beans instead of meat."

As proud as he was, she guessed that Quint hadn't meant to tell her that sometimes he'd gone hungry. Quickly she said, "According to research, beans are better for you than red meat." She smiled ruefully. "Oops. I suppose as the half owner of a ranch, I shouldn't have said that."

"No, you shouldn't have. It's bad for business."

Aileen paused, a celery stalk in her hand. "It just occurred to me that you might not know what your . . . what Jack Bolton looked like."

She rushed into the den. Moments later she returned with two photos in her hand. She placed them on the counter next to Quint. "This one was taken three years ago at a horse show." Aileen looked at the back of the other photo. "In this one he was about your age. You look a lot like him. And it's not just the green eyes."

Quint didn't say anything, but she saw his lips tighten. Aileen resumed preparing the relish tray. From the corner of her eye, she thought she caught him stealing glances at the photographs.

Aileen set the tray on the table. Then she sorted through the junk mail and disposed of it. The rest she set aside when Quint brought their filled bowls to the table. She ate a third of her chili before she spoke.

"This is really good. I appreciate your having dinner ready. It's nice to come home and not have to rush into the kitchen to cook."

"When it looked like it would rain hard all day, I decided that we would work around the place and fix things. That gave me a chance to start dinner. I'm glad you like the chili."

When Quint realized how much her compliment, her smile, warmed him, his mood sobered. It didn't pay to get too attached to anyone or anything. Every time he did, something happened and he had to move on. Except not this time. Now he was no longer a nobody. If he was tenacious enough, he could grab a foothold and put down roots. Deep roots.

"Speaking of fixing things, could you some time go with me to my mentor's house? She's on sick leave this semester and I noticed this morning that the latch of her screen door is broken again. I tried to fix it several weeks ago, but obviously I didn't do it right."

"Sure. No problem. What's she like?"

"Dora's a tough and demanding teacher but fair. She's quick to praise and encourage. The kids respect her. They learn a lot in her classes. She's the reason I became a teacher."

"You like her a lot," Quint observed.

"Yes." Aileen put her spoon down. "So, what did you fix around here?"

"Checking up on me?" Quint asked, trying to keep his voice light.

"No, but I like to know what's going on."

"How's that different from checking up on me?"

"Maybe it's not," she admitted. "We're partners, though, and I don't want to be excluded again. Please remember that."

The fact that Jack never consulted her still rankled. Quint could understand that. "We worked in the tack room, moved the remaining hay to the front of the loft, and tinkered with several machines that we'll be using."

"Which ones?"

"The tractor and everything we'll need to plant alfalfa and clover." Seeing her surprised expression, he added quickly, "It's a lot cheaper to grow your own feed."

"I know that. I'm not criticizing your idea."

"Bob told me that years ago part of the south range was cultivated. I looked at it. Having lain fallow for so long, we should harvest a bumper crop of hay."

"You're full of surprises. Do you know how to plant and harvest?"

"We did it on the spread where I was the foreman. Do you have any objections to me doing this?"

"No, of course not. Go for it."

"I will."

"I remember Mom talking about how they all helped to

get the hay in before it rained. I wonder why they stopped growing it."

Quint had an idea but didn't voice it. She might misunderstand and attribute anything negative he said about Jack to resentment on his part. But he liked the way Aileen looked at him, sort of surprised but pleased as well.

While they did the dishes, they talked about the vegetables she would plant. It was such a pleasant, harmonious evening that tacitly neither referred to the evening before.

Quint excused himself to look at seed catalogues in the den. He studied them until he heard Aileen's laughter, low and throaty. Lured by it as if it were a siren's tempting song, he walked back to the kitchen.

Chapter Six

Quint stopped in the doorway to watch Aileen. She was sitting at the kitchen table, papers spread before her, laughing. Under the overhead light her hair glistened like an alchemist's magic mixture of molten gold and copper. When she became aware of him, she looked up. Her eyes were filled with laughter.

"I'm sorry," she said. "I didn't mean to disturb you."

"You didn't," Quint said, smiling at her. "Care to share what's making you laugh?"

"It's my students. Or rather, their writing." She smothered her laughter before she continued. "We read this Russian short story in which the peasants stage a revolt. So one of my juniors wrote that the pheasants revolted. Can you picture this flock of birds marching on the Winter Palace in St. Petersburg?" Aileen burst into laughter again.

Quint couldn't help but join in, for her laughter was infectious. "Makes you wonder if they had six-shooters or rifles tucked under their wings."

Aileen laughed. When she stopped, she placed her hand

on her chest and caught her breath. "Teaching does have some unusual perks."

The telephone rang.

"Since you're closer, will you get the phone?" Aileen asked.

Quint did. After a moment he asked, "May I ask who's calling?" He placed his hand over the speaker. Looking at Aileen, he mouthed, "Steve?"

"I'll take it." Aileen crossed the room and took the phone from Quint.

"Hi, Steve. What can I do for you?"

Quint opened the refrigerator and studied its contents. He heard her say, "It's no one you know." So, Steve was curious about him. Quint couldn't blame him. If he phoned Aileen and a man answered, he sure as heck would want to know all about him. And do something about him. Was Steve the physical type who'd ask him to step outside and settle it man to man? The part of him that was trying to become a respected rancher hoped not. The part of him that contained the remnants of the fiery-tempered boy who'd been ready to right all affronts with his fists hoped so.

Quint tried not to listen to the conversation, but it was impossible not to hear Aileen's side of it.

He took a bottle of root beer from the fridge and twisted the top off. Aileen's face had lost its humor. He was sure her frown was one of annoyance.

"I'm sorry, but I can't go," she said, her tone firm. "I told you that the other day."

Steve apparently wasn't taking no for an answer. What a jerk.

"Okay, you guessed right. I already have a date," Aileen said, her voice exasperated. "Bye." She hung up forcefully.

Quint watched her press the button to activate the answering machine. She obviously did not want to talk to Steve again. Before he could ask her if anything was wrong, the phone rang again. Ignoring it, she took her seat at the kitchen table. The caller hung up when the recorded message rang through the silent kitchen. Steve, Quint suspected.

"Is something wrong?" Quint asked.

She shrugged.

"Sounds to me like Steve isn't good at taking no for an answer."

"He isn't. I don't know what's gotten into him. In Washington he was insisting on meeting for a drink or sitting beside me on the bus, and now he keeps pestering me for dates. I've run out of excuses."

"Why don't you just tell him you don't want to go out with him," Quint suggested.

"I thought I did. He's either exceptionally dense or—"

"Or he can't believe that you could turn him down. Seems to me the guy has an enormous ego."

"Don't most men?"

"Not me," Quint said, laying his hand on his heart in mock seriousness.

"Yeah, right," Aileen said, trying to sound stern. She placed the papers in a stack. Then she sighed. "Now I have a problem."

"What is it? Maybe I can help."

"I lied when I told Steve I already had a date."

"The guy practically forced you to lie to get rid of him." Quint frowned. "I don't understand. How will he know you lied?"

"When I show up by myself at the National Honor Society dinner. Why couldn't I think of a better excuse?" Aileen said, her voice a discouraged wail. "Now what am

I going to do? Claim my date got sick? He'll never buy that."

"Why don't you just get a date?"

Aileen looked at Quint as if he'd lost his mind. "Get a date? Just like that? By a week from Friday? I told you, I haven't dated since Dad got sick. I don't even know who's available anymore. And it isn't as if this county were over-run with eligible men in the first place."

Quint studied her silently until she asked, "What?"

"You could ask me. I'm available and eligible."

"You?" she asked incredulously.

He raised an eyebrow. "What? A simple cowboy not good enough? Afraid I'll embarrass you? Darlin', I'll have you know, I clean up pretty good."

Aileen's face flushed. She kept forgetting how sensitive he was. "I only meant that you'd be bored stiff. A man like you?"

"What does that mean, a man like me?"

"Well, I'm sure you're used to more exciting dates than the local high school's National Honor Society dinner."

"Depends. What's on the menu?" Quint asked.

"Are you serious?"

"Try me. What's to eat?" he repeated.

"The menu's the same every year. Roast beef. Fried chicken. Mashed potatoes. Green beans. Rolls. Pies. Milk, iced tea, or coffee."

"Cherry pie?"

"Usually, along with apple and a couple of different cream pies."

"Sounds good to me."

Aileen stared at him, wide-eyed. "You're serious?"

"I am. Why not?"

"You'll have to wear a tie," she warned.

"I can handle that."

"And there will be speeches and a short ceremony," she added.

"I'll drink plenty of coffee to keep me awake."

"If you're sure—"

"Aileen, I said I was. I'll escort you to the dinner."

"Thank you," she said gravely, suddenly feeling a little shy.

"You're welcome. Good night."

Aileen was so flustered that she didn't say good night until Quint was already in the hall. Then she sat back, considering what she had just done.

She had just accepted a date with Quint, the man with whom she wasn't going to get involved. Except it wasn't a real date. Quint was just her escort for the evening.

The phone rang again. Aileen tensed until she heard her friend's voice.

"Aileen, pick up. I've got to talk to you. Are you there?"

"I'm here, Jennifer. What's up?"

"I'm calling you from the pay phone in the library. Guess who I've just run into?"

"I have no idea. Brad Pitt?"

"I wish. No, Steve Sanders. He followed me into the children's room and demanded to know who you're going out with. What's up with him?"

"I wish I knew. He seems to think that because I went to Washington as a chaperone, I should go out with him."

"There was a time you thought he had possibilities," Jennifer pointed out. "Of course, that was before Gorgeous Green Eyes arrived on the scene."

Aileen opened her mouth to deny this but then snapped it shut.

"No comeback? I take that as a yes to my question. So, who's your date for the dinner? As if I needed to ask."

"It's not a date," Aileen said.

"Oh? How's it not a date?"

"Well, on a date, the man picks up the woman—"

"Quint isn't picking you up simply because he lives in the same house."

Ignoring Jennifer's statement, Aileen said, "And the couple goes to dinner—"

"Aren't you going to dinner?"

"You know what I mean. This is hardly an intimate, romantic dinner with most of the faculty there and a bunch of students and their parents. And I'm sure you remember the cafeteria? Not even a blind person could claim it was a romantic setting."

"Well, no," Jennifer agreed, "but you're going as a couple and that's what counts."

"We're not a couple. Quint is just my escort."

"Oh, but what an escort. You'll be the envy of every woman there."

Aileen groaned. "Maybe I should come down with some highly contagious disease and stay home."

"You can't do that! My baby sister is being inducted, remember?"

Aileen sighed. "You're right, but I have a bad feeling about this."

"Why? You're taking a date. Most single teachers do and the married ones bring their spouses. It would be odd if you didn't."

"I guess you're right."

"I know I'm right. What are you going to wear?"

"Wear? I hadn't given that any thought yet. Maybe my blue pantsuit."

"No, no. You've got to wear a dress. Show off your legs and flash a hint of cleavage. You know my motto: You got it, flaunt it a little."

"This is a school function, for heaven's sake."

Jennifer sighed. "I know." Then she cheered up. "Hey, you know what? Why don't you and Quint go with us to The Black Hat on Saturday? Do a little dancing. I bet Quint knows how to dance. If not, I'm sure he's a fast learner."

"He's a good dancer."

"Oh? And how do you know that?"

Aileen wished she could retract her rash disclosure.

"Spill it, girl. How do you know that?"

"He waltzed me around the kitchen the other night."

"Oh, really? What else happened?" Jennifer asked, breathless with curiosity.

"Nothing else happened. Listen, I've got to hang up. Haven't finished grading. Bye."

Aileen sat back down, but had a hard time concentrating on the compositions. It didn't help that the phone rang twice more, but when the answering machine message clicked on, the caller hung up. When it rang a third time, she walked toward the phone but couldn't bring herself to pick it up.

Quint came back into the kitchen. Seeing Aileen standing by the phone with a frown, he reached around her and turned the volume dial to its lowest setting.

Aileen smelled soap and a warm, damp male body. He must have just showered. She didn't dare turn around to look at Quint.

"Do you always have such a hard time turning down persistent men?" he asked.

She shrugged. "Steve is a colleague and that makes everything more difficult."

"I don't see why. He's not asking you to help him in a school matter. He's asking you for a date. You turned him down. That's the end of it."

"Would it be for you? I mean, if a woman said no to a date, would you leave it at that?"

"Sure. I'd be disappointed, but I wouldn't bother her again."

"No means no?"

"Absolutely," Quint assured her.

Despite her best intentions not to, Aileen turned around to look at him. Big mistake. He was wearing jeans. He'd left his shirt unbuttoned. Quint had dried himself hurriedly. Water dripped from the ends of his black hair to his shoulders. Unthinking, she reached out to touch a rivulet. Quint caught her hand.

"How does it feel to be that desirable to a man?" he asked.

"To Steve? I suspect it's probably mostly his ego that makes him persistent, not my appeal."

"Don't be too sure of that," Quint murmured. "For a prim schoolmarm, you pack quite a wallop in the appeals department."

"And if I weren't a schoolmarm, I'd be—"

"Still sexy. In a ladylike way."

"Isn't that an oxymoron?" When she saw his raised eyebrow, she said, "Sorry. That's the English teacher speaking. An oxymoron is a sort of contradiction."

"Meaning that a woman is either sexy or a lady but never both?"

Aileen nodded. "There's a long tradition in literature that depicts women as either a madonna or a whore."

"That's narrow-minded thinking," Quint said, "and wrong. Just about every woman is a combination of both. It depends on the situation which part dominates."

Quint had entwined their fingers. He turned their hands so that hers rested against his chest. He moved it slowly across his warm skin. His chest hair caressed her like raw silk. Aileen felt her heartbeat thunder in her ears. A warning, or the bewitching beat of a jungle drum? Both, probably. After a moment's hesitation, she tugged to free her hand. Quint let it go.

"The madonna's voice was apparently louder," he murmured.

"Ours is a working relationship, so it's best," she claimed.

"You're probably right," Quint replied, his tone reluctant, grudging. He left the kitchen before he could be tempted into disagreeing with Aileen.

The sun was close to disappearing behind the horizon when Aileen straightened up and leaned on her rake. A moment later she pressed her hand against her back.

"Sore?" Quint asked, joining her.

"Yes. I guess our aerobic sessions don't hit all the muscles I use in getting the garden ready for planting."

"Sure looks good," Quint said, looking at the neat, rectangular beds Aileen had laid out. "You put in a lot of work. Did you have to do it all this weekend?"

She nodded. "Next weekend it might rain and then it would be a little late to plant the early vegetables."

"Which are?"

"Spinach, sweet peas, and some lettuces, and greens. They like the cool growing season."

"Like clover and alfalfa," Quint said.

"Exactly. That's why you worked every day this week until it was too dark to see."

"It's been a hard week, but good. Got the planting done."

Aileen heard the satisfaction and the pride in his voice. Who would have thought that Quint would turn into such a hard worker? Not she, certainly. At least not that first afternoon when he'd come to the ranch. Her father had done the right thing in giving half of the ranch to Quint. Not only had it been morally the right thing to do, but right from a purely practical point of view as well. She would never have found a foreman who was even remotely as dedicated to the ranch as Quint was.

If only she didn't find him so disturbingly appealing. So far one of them had always remembered that getting involved was a bad idea. They needed cool heads and friendly cooperation to keep the ranch going. What if they both forgot that at the same time? Heaven help them. Resolved to keep a strong rein on her emotions, she turned toward the house.

"I better go in and check on dinner. I put the meat into the crock pot after lunch and the vegetables into the oven an hour ago."

"Sounds good to me. I'll put the tools away for you," he offered.

When Quint joined Aileen in the kitchen, she was poking the meat with a fork. He walked up behind her to look over her shoulder. "Looks and smells good."

"It's just about ready. Are you hungry?"

"Always." And not just for food. Standing this close, his entire body hummed with awareness of her. As if she sensed something, she moved away. "What can I do to help?"

"Take the meat out and put it on this platter." Aileen handed him the dish and then turned her attention to putting the vegetables on the table.

They concentrated on their food, the way people do who work hard physically and need to replenish their strength.

When the dishes were done, Aileen lifted and lowered her shoulders with a grimace.

"Just how sore are you?" Quint asked. Without waiting for an answer, he placed his hands on her shoulders and began to massage them.

Aileen gripped the edge of the counter. She couldn't re-press a groan of pain.

"I know it hurts at first, but soon the pain will lessen considerably. I know. Whenever I could afford it, I'd get a massage after rodeoing."

"Really?"

"Uh-huh."

"By a man or a woman?"

"Whichever was available. These were professionals. Not the people who work in the sleazy massage parlors you're thinking about."

"How do you know I was thinking of massage parlors?"

"From the tone of your voice. It went all teachery."

"It did not! And there's no such word as 'teachery.' "

He grinned at her. "I was bracing myself for lunch detention," he murmured into her ear.

"I bet you served plenty of those."

Quint chuckled. He bet most of her male students didn't much mind serving lunch detention in her classroom. He certainly wouldn't. Given the choice between feasting his eyes on her or his stomach on school cafeteria food, he'd choose Aileen every time. She had shifted her position slightly, bringing her closer to him. By leaning forward just a little, his lips brushed against her hair, which smelled of sunlight and spring air.

Aileen closed her eyes. Quint had been right. The pain had passed into something resembling pleasure. She gripped the counter harder and bit her lower lip to keep from purring with delight.

Somehow she must have communicated her pleasure, for suddenly she felt Quint's body touching hers. The temptation to lean against him was immense. With a last clutch at reality, Aileen took a couple of steps away from him.

"Thanks, but I better go and stand under a hot shower. I'll see you in the morning." Aileen left quickly.

Quint leaned against the counter. Was one of them always destined to flee from this kitchen?

Aileen gathered her hair into her right hand, attempted to smooth it with her left prior to coiling it, and, failing to do so, finally let it fall with a frustrated grimace.

She must have successfully swept up her hair hundreds of times in her life, so why was she having so much trouble tonight? Bracing her hands against the top of her dressing table, she stared at herself in the mirror.

This was her third time attending the National Honor Society dinner. Actually, her fourth, if she counted her own induction. She didn't have to do anything but read the students' names as they came forward to be recognized, so why did her stomach feel as if it had been invaded by a swarm of high-strung butterflies?

"Aileen? I don't mean to rush you, but shouldn't we be leaving soon?" Quint called from the bottom of the stairs.

She opened her bedroom door. "I'll be down in five minutes."

"Okay. Want me to drive?"

"Sure."

"My pickup or your car?" Quint asked.

"My car gets better gas mileage. The keys are on the hall table."

Having promised to be ready in five minutes, Aileen sprang into action. Miraculously, her hair coiled neatly on the next attempt and her fingers were steady while applying eyeliner and lip gloss. She made it downstairs in four minutes.

Quint was waiting for her in the hall. Aileen didn't know if the sight of him or her mad rush down the stairs had made her breathless. Wearing gray slacks, a navy jacket, and a white shirt with a discreetly patterned tie, he wouldn't be out of place in any social situation in the county. Or the state, or—

"Will I do?" he asked with an amused expression.

He had caught her staring! She was glad she had been only staring rather than drooling. He certainly looked good enough to be gazed at covetously, breathlessly, adoringly. She tried to imagine what it would feel like to trace those high cheekbones, to kiss that smiling mouth, to. . . . Aileen felt heat rise all the way to her coiled hair. Reining in her wayward thoughts, she murmured, "You were right. You clean up nicely."

"Well, thank you, ma'am," he drawled. "You don't look half bad yourself. This . . . color looks terrific on you."

Picking up on his brief hesitation, she asked, "This . . . color? I always tell my students to be precise. What would you call the color of my dress?" She softened the challenge in her voice with a smile.

Quint took the opportunity to let his eyes travel lazily from her high-heel-clad feet to the top of her hair. He tried to keep his gaze from lingering too long on her dress. Not that it was too low cut. But ordinarily she wore such buttoned-up, schoolmarmish clothes that this dress took his breath away. It showed off her slender, creamy neck. He swallowed a couple of times.

"The color of my dress?" she prompted.

He rubbed his freshly shaved chin. "You got me. Well, it's obviously blue, but beyond that, I don't know what to call the color. Except . . ."

"Except? Go on."

"As I think back, almost every Madonna in every Mexican church I've been in wore a mantle of that color."

"Very good! Madonna blue is descriptive and evocative," she told him, her voice delighted.

"Yeah? Do I get an A?" he asked with a grin.

His sexy grin definitely merited an A. Quint took a step closer and righted the pendant on her chain. Those pesky butterflies picked up the tempo of the dance.

"Do I get an A?" he repeated softly.

"Possibly. If the rest of the writing measured up."

"I knew it. You're a tough grader."

"Have to be. Otherwise the kids get lazy." Just like her voice, which had sunk to a low murmur.

"Lazy?" Quint asked, his voice husky. He was still touching the pendant.

"Lazy, as in they don't bother to think, and I get a lot of blah words like nice, cute, okay, cool." She felt that if he didn't move his finger, she might do something fatally unwise, like melting against him and begging him to kiss her or just grabbing him and kissing him with shameless abandon.

Quint stepped back. "I think we better go."

Chapter Seven

T hey arrived at the school at the last moment, escaping the obligatory mingling that preceded the dinner. Small talk never counting among her favorite pastimes, Aileen was glad to have been spared the pre-dinner chatter.

The committee in charge of the event had made an attempt to turn the functional cafeteria festive, with white paper tablecloths and pots of red and white geraniums. A sophomore, acting as usher, led them to one of the front tables. Aileen felt as if every eye in the place watched them walk across the cafeteria.

Aileen introduced Quint to Dora and the rest of the people at their table: Sam Jensen, chairman of the school board and feed-store owner, his wife, Myrtle, and two sets of proud parents and their inductees.

The ladies of the cafeteria served the meal family-style, and although talk was general while they passed the various bowls and platters, Aileen steeled herself for the inevitable question about Quint. When it came, its lack of subtlety surprised her.

"So, Quint, what line of work are you in?" Sam Jensen asked.

Everyone at the table stopped chewing, or so it appeared to Aileen. Before Quint could respond, she said, "Quint is the new half owner of the Triangle B."

Sam Jensen's mouth hung open for a second before the usually smooth-talking board member recovered from his surprise. "Well, I'll be. Jack Bolton would have sooner parted with his right hand than an inch of that land. He must be rolling over in his grave."

"I doubt that," Aileen said. "It was his idea."

Sam's deep-set eyes studied Quint. "You knew Jack?"

"In a manner of speaking. He was my father."

The absolute silence that followed Quint's announcement hung heavily over the table.

"Then you and Aileen are brother and sister?" Myrtle Jensen asked.

"No, Mrs. Jensen, Quint and I are not related at all. The Boltons adopted me," Aileen explained.

"Oh."

Myrtle Jensen's mouth formed a perfect circle. Her small nose twitched like a rabbit's having caught an interesting scent. Aileen prepared herself to be interrogated.

"And you're living at the ranch?" Myrtle asked Quint.

"Of course he lives at the ranch," Dora interjected in her best teacher's voice. "You can't run a ranch from town. Even you, Myrtle, ought to know that."

Aileen didn't miss the narrowed eyes and the pursed mouth. The school board member's wife suspected that she and Quint were sleeping together. Remembering the charged scene before they left for the dinner, Aileen had to admit that Myrtle's intuition wasn't that far off the mark.

If Quint hadn't kept his head. . . . Aileen trembled to think of what might have happened.

"Looks like the program is about to begin," Dora said, effectively cutting off whatever else Myrtle had planned to ask.

When the ceremony ended and Aileen had congratulated the inductees and their parents, she went into the gym.

The junior class had decorated the gym with paper flowers, streamers, and balloons. They had even swathed the bright ceiling lights with white gauze, bathing the huge room in a gentle, diffused light.

The DJ's music made conversation difficult. Quint bent down to ask Aileen, "Can we dance?"

She shook her head. She cupped her hand around her mouth and spoke into his ear. "Not yet. We are chaperones for the first hour." Aileen hadn't noticed how shapely his ear was. She felt the crazy desire to nibble on his earlobe. And then trail kisses along his throat—

"What exactly are we looking for as chaperones?" he asked.

"Somebody spiking the punch. Incipient arguments. Couples smooching in the shadowy corners."

"Seems a shame to interfere with young love."

"Might be more a case of raging hormones," she replied.

Quint could identify with those. It took considerable willpower not to drag Aileen into one of those shadowy corners and steal a few kisses. Ever since he'd seen the undisguised admiration in her eyes when she'd come down the stairs, he'd had to concentrate hard on not staring at her with eyes that revealed his attraction.

"Let's circulate," she said.

Quint stayed by her side as they moved around the gym for the next hour.

When they were relieved by the gym teacher and his

wife, Quint made a quick grab for Aileen's hand and led her onto the dance floor. Even if she had wanted to pull away, she doubted that Quint would have let her. And she did want to dance with him.

The first two dances were fast. Aileen felt as if her pulse echoed the throbbing thump of the drums. Her senses hummed, her body felt light—almost liquid—as she moved to the seductive cadence of the music. They didn't touch each other except with their eyes.

The third number was a slow, soft ballad of yearning and love. Even though Aileen knew it would be prudent to leave the dance floor, she hesitated, and, hesitating, she found herself promptly wrapped in Quint's arms. She had noticed earlier how tightly the couples held each other during the slow dances. Almost as if their bodies were fused together.

"Quint," she said. "Quint? Don't you think you're holding me too close?"

"No. This is the perfect music for slow dancing, and you can't dance to this beat if you're a foot apart."

"I wasn't talking about a foot, but how about a couple of inches? I *am* a teacher, and I don't think—"

"You think too much. I believe I've mentioned that before? Relax, Aileen. Listen to the rhythm of the music and go with it. Enjoy it."

If anything, Quint held her even tighter. Aileen knew she couldn't win this argument short of making a scene. She didn't want to make a scene. Actually, if he'd given her the space she asked for, she probably would have been a little disappointed. And she was enjoying herself.

She'd never known that something as simple as dancing could be so pleasurable, so sensuous. Except dancing wasn't really simple. Hadn't she read somewhere that it was originally a part of the mating ritual? Best not to think about that. Aileen closed her eyes, but that only made her other senses more receptive. She felt Quint's breath feather against her temple. She inhaled his scent, which wove itself around her like a magic circle.

When the music stopped, she murmured an excuse and hastened to the ladies' room. She needed to douse her face with cold water.

The two girls drying their hands apparently hadn't noticed Aileen's entrance.

"I had no idea Ms. Bolton could dance like that," the brunette said. "So sexy!"

"Speaking of sexy. Did you get a good look at her date?" the redhead asked.

"Oh yeah. Isn't he to die for? I could hardly keep my eyes off him," the brunette said, her expression dreamy. "Especially when they were dancing."

"He looks a little like Antonio Banderas, only even more handsome. Where did she find him? Think we could ask Ms. Bolton if he has any brothers?" the redhead asked. "There sure is nobody like him at school. He's so hot!"

"I quite agree with you," Aileen said with a smile when the girls became aware of her. "And he doesn't have a brother. Sorry." Both girls blushed crimson, stammered several embarrassed excuses, and sidled out past Aileen.

Aileen washed her hands and dabbed her hot face with a wet paper towel. Then she rejoined Dora and Quint.

Taking one look at Aileen, Dora asked, "What's the matter?"

"I just realized that by tomorrow, Quint's ownership of half the ranch will be all over town," Aileen said with a sigh.

"Wrong," Dora said and grimaced. "Knowing Myrtle Jensen the way I do, it'll be all over the county before midnight."

"Great," Aileen murmured.

"She's one of my failures. She was in my homeroom for four years. I tried to instill a little tact in her and develop some character, but here clearly nature triumphed over nurture. Her mother was a brainless chatterbox and gossip too, may she rest in peace. Well, we can't win them all," Dora said, patting Aileen's shoulder. "Here's my ride."

They said their good nights in the parking lot. Hugging Aileen, Dora whispered, "Your description of Quint didn't do him justice. He's not only handsome, he's intelligent and, I suspect, passionate and caring. He just might be a keeper."

On the way back to the ranch, Aileen was silent. Quint stole glances at her, trying to gauge her mood. Finally he asked, "Did I do something wrong? Disgrace you in some way?"

"No, of course, not. What makes you ask that?"

"Your silence. You seem to be fretting about something."

"Not fretting, exactly."

"Then what, exactly?"

"I'm not sure. I'm uneasy. I didn't like the way Myrtle Jensen kept looking at us," Aileen admitted.

"As if she wondered if we shared a bed?"

Aileen felt heat shoot into her face. "You had that feeling, too?"

"It was written all over her. I wondered if she was going to find a way to ask us straight out."

"If the program hadn't started when it did, she might have. I bet half of my students there tonight wondered the same thing."

"Only half?" Quint asked, trying to interject some humor into the situation. "I must be getting old." He studied her reaction. Aileen's face was grave. "Aileen, I was joking."

"I know."

"What else is making you so uneasy?" he asked.

"A guilty conscience, maybe?"

"You have nothing to feel guilty about. We've done nothing wrong," Quint insisted.

Not yet, that small voice in her mind whispered.

Quint watched her clench her hands. "But you don't like being gossiped about," he guessed shrewdly.

"I don't. Besides that, I'm a teacher. My behavior is supposed to be exemplary."

"From where I'm sitting, it is. And anybody who says differently will have to deal with me."

Judging by the set of his chin and mouth, Quint meant that. Aileen had never had a man offer to fight in her defense. "You make me feel like some noble lady whose honor has been maligned."

"You are a lady," he said softly. "And a lovely, intelligent woman."

Aileen leaned forward to see his expression.

"What?" he asked, meeting her gaze. "That wasn't a line, if that's what you're wondering about."

"It wasn't?"

"I'm not going to use lines on you."

"That's good." Then why did she feel just a twinge of disappointment? Because she suspected Quint might come up with some sweet nothings that could bewitch a woman? Since when did she yearn for honeyed little lies?

"We're partners. You deserve the truth," Quint said.

Partners. Of course. She couldn't keep forgetting that. What was it Dora had said about the truth? That it was overrated and disillusioning? Her mentor was a wise woman.

At the ranch, Aileen picked up the mail she hadn't had

time to look at before the dinner. She sat at the kitchen table to read it.

Quint picked up the newspaper and joined her.

"What on earth?" she exclaimed, frowning at a letter.

Hearing the alarm in her voice, Quint looked up from the paper. Aileen's face had lost its color. "What's the matter?"

"This is a letter from the Internal Revenue Service. It refers to the tax return filed last year." Wordlessly she handed it to him.

Quint read it. "How can the ranch owe this much money in taxes to the IRS? I don't understand."

"That makes two of us." She shook her head. "I do my own tax return, but that's straightforward and simple. I have no idea what all's involved in figuring taxes that include a payroll, retirement accounts, depreciation on equipment, and heaven knows what else. Do you?"

"Not really. My taxes are little more complicated because I itemize my rodeo expenses, but that's nothing like what you have to file for an outfit the size of the Triangle B. Did Jack do the taxes himself?"

"I'm sure he didn't. He disliked all paperwork." Aileen glanced at the clock before reaching for the telephone. "I'm calling the accountant's secretary. She gave me her home number in case we had any questions."

"And do we have questions," Quint muttered.

"This is Aileen Bolton. I hope I'm not calling too late, but we—" Aileen listened. "Thank you. I received a letter from the IRS. They claim that the Triangle B owes twenty-five thousand dollars more for last year."

Quint watched as Aileen listened to the secretary. At one point he saw her eyes widen and saw her slump against the counter. He took a couple of steps toward her.

"Thank you," Aileen said. "I'll get in touch with the firm that handled the taxes."

After she hung up, Quint said, "From your reaction, I take it that the news isn't good."

Aileen sighed. "Two years ago, Dad took all the paperwork to a firm that specializes in taxes. Mr. Holloway, according to his secretary, is conservative. The tax service, on the other hand, has a reputation for being creative. They always promise big savings in their ads."

Quint frowned. "Creative? What does that mean?"

"I suspect it means looking for loopholes that may or may not be legal. I can't believe Dad fell for their promises."

Aileen looked so bewildered, disappointed, and miserable that Quint wanted to take her in his arms and hold her. Stroke her bright hair. Inhale that caramel-sweet scent that made him hungry for things lost long ago or forever unattainable.

"Why would he?" she asked.

"Sounds to me like the actions of a man in trouble."

Aileen continued as if she hadn't heard him. "I always thought Dad was honest and honorable. But apparently I didn't know him at all. First you and now this. We lived in the same house for a quarter of a century, and I have no idea who he was!"

Quint laid his hands on her shoulders and squeezed gently. When she raised her face to look at him, he saw tears glisten in her eyes.

"I'm sorry," he said simply. "I know it's tough when somebody disappoints us. Especially if we care about that person."

"I should have guessed that something was wrong."

"How?"

"By lots of small things. Like when I first got my job,

we split payments of the household expenses. Then I noticed that he was no longer depositing money into that account, so I started to pay everything." Aileen shook her head. "Even before that, there were plenty of signs, but I didn't interpret them correctly."

"What signs?"

"When I started college, he gave me spending money. The summer after my freshman year I took part in a special research project that paid a very nice stipend. After that, he no longer offered spending money. That was okay. I got a part-time job in the library."

"What else? You said there were plenty of signs."

"Halfway through my sophomore year, he asked me to live at home and commute. That surprised me because the campus wasn't all that close. He claimed that the cleaning woman wasn't doing a good job anymore."

"Now you think these things were signs that the ranch wasn't doing well?"

"I'm not sure, but what else could they mean?"

"Maybe he was lonely and missed you and wanted you back home," Quint suggested.

"I wish!"

"Explain that."

"Looking back over the years, he never seemed to want my company. When Dad came to my school functions, which wasn't often, I'm pretty sure it was because Mom absolutely insisted. After her death we hardly spent any time together, even after I moved back home."

"Maybe he thought you needed the time to study."

"I did, but every single evening? In retrospect, the only reason for his asking me to live at home had to be financial." Aileen frowned. "Are you defending him?"

Quint chuckled without humor. "The sun won't rise on the day I defend Jack Bolton. Trust me on that."

"Then why are you trying to make me think better about him? Make me think he cared about me?"

"Because I cannot imagine that he couldn't care about you. Me, he didn't know, so it was easy not to care about me, but you?" Quint shook his head.

"You're trying to make me feel better. Thanks, but it isn't necessary," she claimed, knowing that this wasn't true. Deep down she still yearned for her father's love, just as she had always yearned for his approval.

"So, what are we going to do about this IRS bill?" she asked, needing to change the subject. "I don't have twenty-five thousand dollars lying around."

"I don't either."

"Which means we have to borrow the money. You agree?"

"I hate to borrow money, but I don't see what other choice we have."

"I'll make an appointment with the banker."

After school on Monday, Aileen met Quint at the bank.

Greetings and pleasantries exchanged, the vice president asked, "What can I do for you?"

Aileen explained their tax situation.

"Are you requesting a second mortgage on the ranch?" the bank officer asked.

Aileen stared at the man for several heartbeats before she was able to process this devastating statement. "What do you mean, a *second* mortgage? There hasn't been a mortgage on the Triangle B in . . . I don't know how long."

"Actually, never. Not until Jack Bolton mortgaged the place four years ago," the vice president said. "I'd advise against taking on a second mortgage. If you can manage to pay the IRS any other way, do it."

"Why on earth did he take out a mortgage?" Aileen asked, her voice shaky, her expression bewildered.

"He told me he'd started to play the stock market and didn't do so well."

Aileen barely repressed a despairing moan.

"How big is the mortgage?" Quint asked.

She heard the sum and swayed as if poleaxed. Aileen suspected that only Quint's steadying hand on her arm kept her from sliding out of her chair in a dead faint. In a daze she heard the men discuss the mortgage, refinancing, interest rates, and other options, such as drilling for oil.

Drilling for oil? The words penetrated Aileen's numb mind. "That's not an option," she said. "Absolutely not. Mom always opposed the idea of despoiling the land. I do too."

"And I'm not in favor of a second mortgage," Quint said. "How about you, Aileen?"

She shook her head. "Only as a last resort."

"Then we'll have to come up with other options."

Before they left, the vice president assured them that if he could be of service, they should call him.

Aileen seemed to be in a state of near shock. Without hesitation, Quint led her to Ruby's Cafe down the street. He steered her to a table by the window.

The waitress set down two glasses of water. "You folks want coffee?"

"Yes, and bring us two pieces of apple pie with ice cream," Quint said.

He studied Aileen's face. It seemed drained of all color.

"How could he do that? Mortgage the ranch? After Mom repeatedly told about how several local ranchers during the Depression lost their land because they'd mortgaged it? She would sooner have sold herself on the streets of Cheyenne than have taken out a mortgage."

The waitress brought their order. As soon as she left, Aileen continued in the same tortured, stunned tone. "What possessed him to play the stock market? He knew nothing about it. Dad was a rancher, for heaven's sake. Though I'm beginning to think he wasn't a good one."

"Seems to me Jack was a desperate man. He hadn't done well with the ranch, so he thought he'd recoup his losses by playing the stock market," Quint said.

"Then why not go to a reputable stockbroker?"

"That would be like admitting that he wasn't . . . perfect?" Quint shrugged. "I didn't know him, so that's only a guess."

"It's a fairly accurate guess. He liked everything to be perfect." She pressed the palms of her hands against her forehead. "I don't believe any of this!"

"Aileen, eat your pie."

"I don't think I can."

"Yes, you can. I'm not having you pass out on me." Quint picked up her fork, scooped up some pie and ice cream, and held it out to her. "Eat."

"I'm not going to faint."

"I'll believe that when you get some color in your face. Now eat. This is first-class pie." He kept holding the fork until, with a sigh, she let him place the food into her mouth. "Good girl. Just a few more bites."

Aileen rolled her eyes. "Give me that fork," she said, half amused, half ticked-off.

"Not until you promise to eat."

"How can I, with the IRS breathing down our neck? You know they take people's property in payment for back taxes? We could lose the ranch!"

"We won't."

"And you know exactly how we're going to prevent that?"

"Maybe. With your help, we can figure this out. Look at the last form in the envelope the IRS sent."

"Why?" Aileen asked, even as she was taking the envelope from her handbag.

"I think there was a section asking how much the initial payment was going to be and how much we could pay monthly."

"The Internal Revenue Service has an installment plan?" Aileen asked, her voice disbelieving. She flipped to the section Quint had mentioned. "I can't believe this! You were right!" Aileen rooted through her bag until she found a pen. On the back of the envelope she feverishly wrote columns of numbers.

"What are you doing?"

"Listing our monthly living expenses to see how much we need and how much we could pay out of my salary."

"Aileen, I can't let you do this alone."

"You're not. The profit from the ranch, which will largely depend on you, will be responsible for the mortgage payments, the salaries and insurance premiums for the hands, property taxes, etcetera, etcetera. So you see, you'll contribute more than your share."

"Well, if you put it that way—"

"I do put it that way because that's the way it is." Aileen pushed the envelope toward him. "The circled figure is the amount we can send the IRS every month. Below that is how much I can take from my savings account for the initial payment."

Aileen picked up her fork and started to eat. Surprised, she said, "This is excellent pie and ice cream."

"I told you it was." Quint studied the figures. "I can match the amount for the first payment."

"Are you sure? I don't want you to be caught short."

"I can get by with very little, as long as you feed me."

"No problem." Aileen scraped up the last bit of pie. Then she stopped, dismayed. "Oh no! I've eaten the whole thing! First I skipped aerobics because of the bank appointment, and now I consumed hundreds of extra calories. My hips will spread and spread, and it's all your fault."

"And I have the perfect solution."

"What?" she asked, seeing the sparkling light in his green eyes. He leveled one of his sexy grins at her. Aileen could feel her toes curl. "What's your solution?"

He took her hand and entwined their fingers. "Tonight I'll waltz you around the kitchen. Dancing burns lots of calories. When we get tired of waltzing, I'll teach you to rumba, mamba, and samba. Maybe even to polka."

"You know how to polka?" she asked, suppressing a grin.

"Don't laugh. The polka is a lot of fun."

"If you say so," she said, smiling at him. With her peripheral vision she saw someone stop at their table.

"Sam, look who's here."

It couldn't be Myrtle Jensen, Aileen thought, but it was. Guiltily she tried to tug her hand from Quint's. He wouldn't let her.

"Good evening, Mrs. Jensen, Mr. Jensen. How are you?" Quint asked in a calm, conversational tone. "We'd ask you to join us, but we were just leaving." He let go of Aileen's hand to reach for the check. "Excuse us."

"Nice to see both of you," Aileen murmured and followed Quint to the cashier's station by the door. She felt Myrtle's speculative, triumphant, malevolent glance follow her all the way.

Chapter Eight

"I didn't think the day could get any worse, but I was wrong," Aileen said when she arrived at the ranch right after Quint. She dumped her briefcase and purse on the hall table and slumped against it dejectedly.

"Are you referring to Myrtle Jensen?" he asked.

"Who else? Did you see that 'Aha! I got you' expression on her face? She caught us holding hands in public and, for her, that's proof of her basest suspicions about us."

"I'm not thrilled about her seeing us holding hands, but it's no big deal." Quint shrugged. "Aileen, aren't you over-reacting?"

"Ordinarily it wouldn't be a big deal, but we live in the same house! That colors everything."

"I suppose it does," Quint said, his expression thoughtful. "But what can she do? Spread gossip? Don't you think people around here know what she's like?"

"Yes, but there will be talk. And then the whole 'where there's smoke, there's fire' mentality will take over. This is a small, rural community."

"Ignore the talk. It's the best approach. Believe me.

Don't get involved in defending or denying anything. If you do that, people will wonder if there's truth to the rumors."

"Maybe you're right," Aileen murmured.

"What do you want to do now? Dance naked around the kitchen?" Quint asked with a mischievous expression.

Aileen rolled her eyes.

"I was only kidding. We need a little humor. How about me saddling up a couple of horses and we go for a ride?"

"No, thanks. What I want to do is go into the den and fill out the forms for the IRS. And go over our finances. Maybe later you can teach me to polka. With our clothes on."

"Darn. You know how to take the fun out of the polka." Quint retreated to the den before she could say anything else.

Aileen made a pot of coffee, filled two mugs, and carried them into the den.

"I haven't gone through all the desk drawers yet. Maybe I can find some of Dad's tax stuff." In the bottom drawer she found a yellowed envelope. She opened it and took out a photo.

"What's that?" Quint asked.

Aileen looked at the back of the photo. "It's labeled, 'Mom, Jack, and Linda.' " She held out the photo for Quint to see. "This could be your grandmother. And Linda could be your aunt. Isn't this exciting?" She watched him shrug and turn his attention back to the papers. "There's no address, so we can't trace them. That's too bad."

Quint ignored her comment, concentrating on last year's monthly reports posted by the accountant. He frowned.

"That bad?" she asked, putting the photo away.

"That puzzling. Run right, the Triangle B should not only break even, but show a decent profit."

"It obviously was profitable while Mom was alive."

Quint leaned back in his chair. "Tell me what it was like back then. Close your eyes and picture the ranch."

Aileen closed her eyes. After a few seconds, she said, "We had chickens. I remember I liked feeding them. And we had two or three milk cows. Even a bunch of pigs. And Mom and Martha put in the biggest vegetable garden you can imagine. All summer long, we canned, froze, dried, and 'put up' food, as Martha called it, to last all winter."

"You already mentioned that you used to plant alfalfa and clover for hay. Bob told me you even grew your own oats for the horses. The ranch was practically self-sufficient."

Aileen nodded. "After Mom died, I remember Dad standing on the porch, giving orders to the men. Before her death, he used to ride out with them. At least most of the time."

"In other words, Jack Bolton didn't like hard work," Quint concluded.

Aileen gasped and touched his hand. "Quint, I'm sorry. He was your biological father. I didn't mean to imply that—"

"I know you didn't. Don't worry about it. And I'm fairly sure I didn't inherit his gene for laziness."

"I'm positive you didn't!"

"Thanks." Quint smiled at her before turning his attention back to the reports. "What's 'Racing, Inc.'?"

"Some horse racing scheme Dad was briefly involved in."

"Horse racing is very expensive and uncertain. It's lots safer to breed good-looking horses for people who want to ride. By the way, Sweepstake has been busy. We should get a nice crop of colts and fillies next spring which we can sell the spring after that."

"That's great. I hope you haven't overexerted him." Aileen felt herself color when she realized what she'd said.

"He loves his work. Hasn't complained once," Quint replied, his voice solemn, but there was a twinkle in his eyes and a quiver around his lips.

"I could say something about the similarities among all males across the species, but I won't." Aileen gestured, dismissing the subject. "Anyway, Racing, Inc. wasn't a total flop. We got several good mares out of the disaster."

Quint turned the page. "What was 'Air Service'?"

"I remember that fiasco. It was a transportation scheme designed to service outlying ranches. It went bankrupt."

"That seems to be the pattern: Jack dreamed up or got sucked into get-rich-quick schemes, all of which lost money. Then he'd borrow more, trying to recoup what he'd lost. That's a sucker's strategy." Quint shook his head.

"At least we know what *not* to do."

Quint leaned forward. For emphasis he touched her hand. "Aileen, if we can hang on for the next two years, we'll survive and start making a profit. But these two years will be tough," he warned.

"I know that. You think I can't hack it, cowboy?"

"I know you can. You're an amazing woman. I just want to be sure that you really want to work that hard and live without frills and luxuries for that long. I need to know that now. Once we start, I don't want to have to quit short of the goal."

"I'm not a quitter." Then, matching his tone in intensity and seriousness, she added, "This is my home. I've always lived here. I'll do anything to keep it." Aileen picked up her mug and raised it. "Here's to two years of simple living and hard work."

"I'll drink to that," Quint said and saluted her.

*   *   *

Before school Aileen thought that some of her colleagues were looking at her speculatively or slyly, but she couldn't be sure. When she entered the teachers' lounge during her prep period for a cup of coffee and all eyes zeroed in on her, she knew she hadn't imagined those glances.

"Wow. Talk of still waters running deep," Janice, the school nurse, said. "All this time I worried about you living like a nun and rapidly becoming a dried-up old maid, and it turns out you've got a hunk stashed away on that ranch of yours."

Maryann leaned forward, her expression eager. "Is he as hot as he looks? Come on, tell all."

Aileen's mouth nearly dropped open. How could Maryann, who had known her for years, assume she'd answer such a question? "On second thought, this coffee looks stale. I think I'll skip it. I've got some grading to do," she murmured and walked out of the lounge.

That afternoon she fled from school the moment the last bell stopped ringing.

As soon as Aileen got to the ranch, she changed clothes and hurried into her garden. One third of the vegetable plot had been roughly tilled. It now needed to be raked into fine soil. She picked up the rake. Nothing like pulverizing clumps of dirt to get over the embarrassing scene in the lounge.

Quint called Aileen's name as soon as he entered the house, but there was no response. Her car was parked in front of the house and her briefcase and purse were on the hall table. The kitchen was empty too. Whatever she had put into the crock pot that morning smelled delicious. His stomach growled in anticipation.

Where was she? Quint walked to the bottom of the stairs and called her name again. He had never been upstairs.

Without ever having discussed it, he knew this was her domain. It would be prudent for him to stay out of it. But what if she was ill? Throwing caution aside, he climbed the stairs two at a time. Since it took her only moments to run down the stairs, he figured that hers had to be the first room off the landing. The door stood partially open. He knocked and called her name.

"Aileen?" He waited a beat and then pushed the door open.

Quint would be the first to admit that he knew nothing about antique furniture, but he was intuitively sure that what he was looking at would qualify as antiques. Beautiful antiques. The dark, polished pieces looked as if they had been made for the room.

Quint had been in enough women's bedrooms to expect a certain amount of frills and fussiness, but aside from the delicate floral wallpaper and the plants on the windowsill, the room was simple, uncluttered, serene. He didn't even see a single stuffed animal. That shouldn't have surprised him. Aileen's room would be classy, like the lady herself. He grinned when he saw the books piled on her night table. There wasn't a room in the house that didn't contain books.

The four-poster bed drew him like a magnet. He picked up the white nightgown that lay folded at the foot of it and raised it to his face. It felt as silky as her hair. He inhaled the scent. Aileen's scent. For a moment he closed his eyes and reveled in the intoxicating sensation. When he realized what he was doing, he hastily but reverently refolded the nightgown with shaky hands and backed out of the room.

Quint tried not to look at the four-poster again, but his traitorous eyes strayed to it. He knew with certainty that from now on that bed would play a prominent role in his heady dreams of Aileen. He groaned. He surely didn't need anything else to rob him of his sleep or to fuel his fevered imagination, or to accelerate the pulsing needs of his body. He muttered a few four-letter words and called himself several unflattering names for having been rash enough to go upstairs.

She had to be in the garden. He rushed outside. Quint heard the thumping noise before he saw her. He stopped and watched her for a moment. The way she smashed the back of the rake down on the clump of earth would have told a blind man that she was upset.

"Do you need any help?" he asked.

She paused. Leaning on the rake, she raised her arm and used her sleeve to wipe the sweat off her forehead.

"You're upset. What happened?"

Thump. She smashed a few more clumps. Quint waited for a moment before he picked up the extra rake and worked on the small clumps until the earth was reduced to black powder, ready to be planted. They worked side by side for several minutes. Finally, he asked, "Are you going to talk to me or keep on smacking these poor clumps?"

Aileen stopped. Facing him, she said, "I can't believe my colleagues. People I've known for years, people who have known me for years, if not for most of my life. You'd think they'd give me the benefit of the doubt. But no. They choose to believe the worst their gutter minds can think of. There isn't a single one who isn't convinced you and I are living in sin."

"Ah." Quint watched her face. She was angry, but beyond the anger he glimpsed disappointment and embarrassment. That riled him enough to want to inflict some serious bodily harm on those who had hurt Aileen's feelings.

He watched her wield the rake forcefully a couple of more times before he laid his hand on her arm to stop her. "What did they actually say?"

"Quint! I'm not going to repeat the innuendos."

He gritted his teeth. "I'm sorry. I didn't anticipate that they'd embarrass you, but this is going to blow over. As soon as something else happens to catch their interest, they'll shift their focus to it."

She sighed. "Probably. The bad thing is that around here not too many exciting things happen, so you and I may be the focal point for a long time."

"Aileen, look at me."

"Why?"

"I need to see your mouth."

"What on earth for?" she asked, thoroughly puzzled.

"To see if it has that much-kissed look."

"What?"

Quint placed his hand under her chin and lifted it. He looked intently at her mouth.

"Why are you looking at me like that?" she managed to ask in a voice that rose barely above a whisper.

"Nope, your mouth has that innocent, virginal look."

Aileen almost jumped out of her gardening clogs. Had he guessed that she was still a virgin? Her glance flew to his face. Relieved, she saw that he was still preoccupied with her mouth. He hadn't noticed her startled reaction. Maybe her mouth having that virginal look didn't mean what she feared it might mean.

"Your colleagues aren't nearly as smart and observant as the think they are. Trust me on that and ignore them."

"That's easier said than done."

"You didn't let them get to you?"

"No. I kept my cool, but just. That's why it was necessary for me to demolish a bunch of clumps."

"You feel better now?"

"Yes," she said, a little surprised. "I do."

"Then let's go inside. It's getting dark. You must have worked up an appetite," Quint said. "And whatever is in the crock pot in the kitchen smells great."

"Oh no! I completely forgot to turn the crock pot off."

Aileen rushed into the house while Quint picked up the tools and set them on the back porch.

"Just as I thought," Aileen said the moment he entered the kitchen. "The meat's falling apart."

She looked defeated, as if this were the last straw. Quint stood next to her and casually draped his arm around her shoulders. He looked into the pot. "Still looks and smells delicious. We could put the meat between pieces of bread. I bet it would taste good," he said encouragingly.

Aileen perked up. "I know what we can do: I'll shred the meat and heat it in some barbecue sauce. You like barbecue sandwiches?"

"Love 'em," Quint said.

"Oh, good. Why don't you get the buns?"

Quint squeezed her shoulder before he did as she asked. Aileen started to wash her hands and let out a cry.

"What's wrong?" he asked, rushing to her side.

"Nothing."

"Yeah, right. Let me see your hands." He turned her hands over and winced. "Weren't you wearing gloves?"

"Yes."

"Didn't you feel the pain? The skin on your palms is rubbed raw."

"I guess I was so upset that I didn't notice the pain."

"We better get your hands cleaned up. Do you prefer soap and water or iodine?" Quint asked.

"Soap and water is fine."

Quint watched her bite her lower lip while he cleaned the raw areas, and although she tried hard not to cry, a couple of tears escaped her eyes. "Hold up your hands to dry," he said. When she did, he placed his arms around her waist. "You've had a hard day, haven't you, darlin'," he murmured. He kissed the tears from her face and drew her closer.

Aileen resisted for a moment before she melted into his arms. It felt so good to be held and fussed over. She sighed and kept her eyes closed.

"I'm tempted to give your dirty-mouthed colleagues a piece of my mind, but it would only make it worse for you. I wish I could do something. I wish——"

Aileen wrenched herself out of his arms and took three steps back.

"Aileen, what's the matter?" he asked, bewildered.

"You can't touch me! Don't you see? If anyone saw us," she said, her panicked glance darting to the window. "The blinds aren't even drawn!" She rushed to the window and tugged on the blind impatiently.

"For heaven's sake! I was only comforting you, not making passionate love to you."

"You know that and I know that, but to anyone else it would not have looked like comforting. We can't give anybody any ammunition against us. No touching of any kind. Agreed?"

"You're overreacting. Nobody is skulking past our kitchen window to spy on us. Okay, okay. I agree," he added quickly, seeing her anxious expression. "But I'm going to have to touch you long enough to put Band-Aids on your hands. All right?"

Mutely she nodded.

Quint mumbled under his breath while he went to fetch the first-aid kit.

The week passed slowly. Aileen kept a low profile, avoiding contact with her colleagues. She steered clear of the teachers' lounge, as if the place smelled to high heaven. She brought her lunch, which she ate at her desk. She left school as soon as she could in the afternoon. Aileen even stopped going to aerobics, choosing to exercise at home. Though she admitted to herself that this was a little cowardly, she just wasn't up to more innuendo-filled encounters.

When she was summoned to the principal's office on Friday after school, she was puzzled. Mr. Russell rarely detained any of the staff on a Friday.

The meeting didn't take long, yet Aileen felt as if she'd received blows to every part of her body. She made her way to her car, barely aware of her actions. Trying to unlock the door, she fumbled. She felt a hand on her shoulder and gasped.

"Quint, you scared me half to death. What are you doing here?"

"Dora phoned. She asked that I meet you here and take you to her place. Come on."

"My car—"

"We'll pick it up on the way home."

Seeing that several people lingered at their cars to watch them, Quint didn't offer her his arm, but he walked close enough that if she needed to, she could lean on him.

She sat still and quiet in the truck, her hands clasped so hard that her knuckles turned white.

Dora must have been watching for them, for she opened the door before Quint had a chance to ring the doorbell.

"Come into the kitchen," Dora said, after taking one look at Aileen's distraught face. "I've got tea brewing."

They followed her into the kitchen.

Aileen sat down at the kitchen table, her back straight, staring at the wall. Quint sat on her right side, Dora on her left.

Quint finally broke the silence. "Will somebody tell me what happened?" He watched Aileen take a deep breath, trying to get control.

"Mr. Russell sent for me."

"The principal," Dora added, for Quint's benefit.

"And what did Mr. Russell say to you?" he asked.

Aileen bit her lower lip. Finally, her voice thick with tears, she said, "The school board is considering the moral turpitude clause."

Quint frowned. "What does that mean?"

"It means that they think I'm a morally reprehensible person. Vile. Base. Shameful and not fit to teach kids. I may lose my job." Aileen burst into tears. She buried her face in her hands and sobbed.

Speechless, Quint laid his hand on her shoulder.

Dora got up and brought a box of tissues, which she set in front of Aileen.

"Can they do that?" Quint asked Dora.

"They might. We never removed that darn clause from the contract," Dora said. "I've served on the negotiation team several times, but we never even talked about that clause. I guess we all thought it was so archaic, so out-moded and ridiculous that it would never be invoked. It was almost a joke." She shook her head, her expression grim.

"I assume this is because we live in the same house?"

Dora nodded.

"Well, I'll pitch a tent and move out."

"I'm afraid it's too late for that," Dora said.

"Then what can we do?" Quint asked.

"Nothing," Aileen wailed. "There's nothing we can do."

"I wouldn't say that," Dora said, handing Aileen a tissue. "We can take them to court. A court battle will be messy and it'll drag on, but it's our best bet. I called my lawyer as soon as I heard, but he'd already left on a fishing trip. Won't be back until next Friday."

"How did you hear?" Aileen asked. "This just happened."

"Joanne called to warn me." Looking at Quint, she added, "Joanne is the assistant principal and a longtime friend." Dora poured the tea and placed a cup in front of Aileen. "Drink this. It'll make you feel better."

"Nothing will ever make me feel better!"

"Nonsense. Blow your nose and drink your tea." Dora's voice rang with authority, the same authority that had forced hundreds of disinterested students to plunge into the annals of American history.

"Why? Why is the school board doing this?" Aileen asked. "It's not as if I were the only one who ever transgressed. What am I saying? I haven't even done any transgressing!" Aileen pressed her hands against her temples.

Quint moved behind her chair. "Here, let me, before you come down with a migraine." He nudged her hands out of the way and gently massaged her temple.

"I would like to know the answer to Aileen's question, too. Why is she being singled out?" he asked.

"I've been wondering about that myself." Dora sipped some tea. "I can come up with several answers. Envy. Jealousy. Resentment. Revenge."

"Are you serious?" Aileen asked, her voice incredulous. "What do I have that anyone could envy? Or what could I have done that anyone would want revenge for?" Aileen asked, her eyes never wavering from her mentor.

Dora sighed. "I could be wrong."

"But you're fairly sure you're not," Quint said. "Is this a hunch, or do you have some evidence for your suspicions?"

"The push to make use of that antiquated clause in the

contract came from one source," Dora said. "Sam Jensen. Or, more accurately, from his wife."

"Myrtle Jensen?" Aileen asked. "I know she's a gossip, but I didn't think there was any real harm in her."

"All gossip isn't necessarily silly or innocent. If you repeat things that are hurtful to people, you can inflict a good deal of pain," Dora said. "And Myrtle doesn't differentiate between frivolous and damaging gossip."

"And she can push her husband into doing things for her? I wouldn't have thought she had that much clout. How does she do it?" Aileen asked.

"Enough whining and nagging can drive most men to do anything," Quint said. "And Myrtle struck me as a whiner and a nagger."

"Good observation," Dora said, with a trace of admiration. "That's exactly how she does it."

Aileen shivered. "But why? I've never done anything to her."

"You haven't, but your mother did, by always being a little smarter, a little prettier, a little more popular. All through high school Myrtle tried to compete with your mother. She always came in second best. Myrtle pretended that she didn't mind, but she did. The final straw was Jack Bolton. He took Myrtle out a few times. Then he met your mother, and three months later he married her."

"But that happened thirty years ago! Nobody can hold a grudge that long," Aileen protested.

"It appears some people can," Dora said.

"I don't believe this is happening!" Aileen whispered.

"Nothing's going to happen this weekend. I want you to go home and put this out of your mind."

"How can I? For all I know, I'll get fired on Monday."

"I don't think so. There has to be at least one school board meeting first. My lawyer, who's an expert on contracts, will be back next Friday. He'll advise us on what to do."

They said their good-byes. Aileen was silent on the drive back to the school parking lot. Quint walked her to her car.

"How's your headache? Are you up to driving home?"

"Yes. Quint, I'm fine," she added, seeing him hesitate.

"Okay. You go on. I'll be right behind you."

Aileen drove slowly, carefully, trying not to think of the enormity of her problem. She didn't quite succeed, but at least she didn't burst into tears and drive off the road.

She waited for Quint on the porch. He walked like a man on a mission. Surprised, she noted that his expression was almost cheerful.

"Let's have a root beer," he said. Quint took her hand and pulled her toward the kitchen.

"Quint, have you already forgotten about the no touching rule?" Aileen tugged, but he refused to let go of her hand.

"Forget about that rule. I have the solution to our problem."

"What? Putting Myrtle Jensen on the next unmanned space flight?"

"Forget about her. What I have in mind will shut up her gossiping mouth once and for all."

"And what's that?"

"Us getting married."

Chapter Nine

Aileen stopped so abruptly she forced Quint to stop as well. Blood rushed to her head and sang in her ears. She couldn't have heard him right.

"What . . . what did you just say?" she asked, her mouth dry, her voice whispery.

"It seems to me there's just one thing to do to solve our present problem: get married."

Her heart hammered so wildly its beat echoed in her temples. "That's what I thought you said," she murmured. He tugged at her hand. Aileen followed him into the kitchen. She had no choice, for surprise and confusion were crushing her ability to think.

"Sit down, please." Quint pulled out a chair and held it for her.

Still in a daze, Aileen sat. Thoughts raced through her head faster than she could process them. Marriage? To Quint? She felt heat rush to every part of her body. Then she shivered as if struck by an icy blast.

"Drink this," Quint said, placing a can of root beer in front of her. He sat, facing her, his expression grave. "I know this idea caught you by surprise. It did me too. I almost drove off the road when it first hit me. But the longer I've been considering it, the more sense it makes."

Aileen stared at him. She met the serious gaze of his stunning green eyes and couldn't have uttered a word if her life had depended on it.

"Think about it, Aileen. Once we're married, no one can object to us living in the same house. It'll be expected. It would be odd if we didn't."

Aileen moistened her dry lips. "Isn't getting married an extreme solution?"

"No, not after you've thought about it. What other choices do we have?" he asked. "As I see it, you could resign before the school board can invoke that dumb moral turpitude clause."

"No! That would be like admitting that I've done something wrong, and I haven't. I won't resign."

Seeing her agitation, Quint laid his hand on hers soothingly. "Okay. You could let them fire you and fight the dismissal. Maybe you'd win and maybe you wouldn't. How can they prove that we're sleeping together? How can we prove that we're not?"

"This isn't anything that can be proved one way or another, is it?" Aileen closed her eyes and shook her head. "The whole thing is insane!"

"When it comes right down to it, I'm afraid that most people will find it easier to believe that we have an improper relationship than that we don't. After all, we share a house; we're both young, healthy, and unattached." Most men, Quint knew, would think there was something seriously wrong with him if he didn't make the moves on Aileen.

Aileen sighed and buried her face in her hands.

"And while we're waiting for the legal process to take

its course, you'd be out of a job. To meet our financial obligations, including payments to the IRS, we'd have to sell a chunk of land."

Aileen quickly raised her head. "No! That's not an option."

He nodded in agreement. "We could try getting a second mortgage, but without your salary, I'm not sure the bank would consider it. Are there any jobs around here you could get quickly that offered a similar salary and benefits?"

"No."

"I rest my case. I can't come up with any other options. Can you?"

"No." Aileen shook her head. "It's just that marriage is such an extreme step."

They both sat in silence, thinking. Finally, Quint asked, "Are you opposed to marriage in principle?"

"No. I always thought I'd get married some day."

"So it's only marriage to me that you find so hard to swallow? Marriage to the illegitimate son of Jack Bolton and a poor migrant girl? Marriage to a man who hasn't been to college, who works with his hands. In short, a man who isn't good enough for you."

She heard the hard edge in Quint's voice, saw the bitter little smile around his lips, and realized that once again she had forgotten his fierce pride. "You misunderstood me. I meant that marriage to anybody is a big step. And speaking of being illegitimate—I'm adopted, remember? My parents were a couple of teenaged kids who got carried away by their hormones. The only difference between us is that your birth mother decided to keep you and mine didn't. So don't talk to me about being illegitimate."

"I hadn't thought of it that way," Quint admitted quietly.

Aileen took a deep breath. "I never imagined I'd get married for such a practical and cold-blooded reason."

"Keeping your home is practical, but cold-blooded?"

"Well, no, not exactly, but—"

"But you thought when a man proposed marriage there would be moonlight and roses and wine and romance."

She glanced at his face to see if he was mocking her. He didn't seem to be. "I think most women would expect that. Don't men?"

He grinned. "I suspect with men it's more physical . . ."

"Sex, you mean."

Quint raised an eyebrow at her dismissing tone. "Never underestimate the power of sex. It's one of the strongest urges around." Judging by the pink color in her cheeks, she hadn't yet considered that aspect of marriage. Quint quickly changed the subject. "Why don't you give this marriage idea some thought? If you come up with a better solution, I'll listen." Quint picked up his root beer and headed for the door. "I have some chores to do. See you at supper."

Aileen watched him leave, the expression on his handsome face almost cheerful, the stance of his body oozing confidence and determination. How could he be so sure that getting married was the right thing to do?

Had they considered all possibilities? Mentally Aileen listed all her assets. Discouraged, she realized that, even if she sold everything dear and of value in the house, the money would not go far. Selling part of the land was not an option, as they needed every acre to make the ranch successful. A loan. Even if they could secure one, how could they repay it without her salary? She needed her job. That was the bottom line. And getting married appeared to be the only way to keep it.

Marrying Quint. Aileen's hand shook as she reached for her drink. What kind of marriage did he envision? She had always expected to be in love with the man she married.

Madly, hopelessly, totally in love. Had Quint hoped for love too?

He did say that men were more practical. Maybe he pictured their marriage merely as a practical arrangement. They would work side by side. They would be partners and companions. Maybe even friends. That was a lot more than many people had, and under the circumstances, such an arrangement was reasonable. It *was*. Then why did she feel so let down, so disappointed?

Aileen shook her head as if to clear it. There was no sense in brooding about the possibilities. She would have to discuss the kind of marriage he wanted. But how? How could she bring up the subject delicately? What kind of marriage did *she* want? She didn't know. That was the problem. She closed her eyes and sighed.

"Oh, grow up and handle it," she told herself. Aileen rose, determined not to think about anything except fixing dinner.

She didn't quite succeed, but she did manage to put a meal on the table. Quint seemed to find it eminently edible, even if she could do little more than stare at her food.

"This is good," he said, taking a second piece of fish. "Aren't you hungry?"

"I guess not."

"Worried?"

"A little. Aren't you?"

Quint ignored her question. "Did you come up with an alternate plan?" he asked.

"No."

"Then we're getting married."

She merely nodded, for her mouth felt full of cotton, making speech impossible.

"You agree we should do it as soon as possible?"

Aileen nodded again.

"How does Wednesday sound to you?" Quint saw the color fade from her face. "I don't mean to rush you, but I thought the whole idea was to beat the school board to the draw. You know, act before they do. Like the military executing a preemptive strike. Was I wrong in assuming that?"

She shook her head.

"Can you take Wednesday off?"

Aileen nodded. She moistened her lips. "I have a personal day left I can take."

"Good. Here's what we'll do. We'll drive to the county seat, buy a license, and go to the justice of the peace for the ceremony. I guess I better call and make an appointment."

"You have it all figured out. Have you done this before?"

"Me? No. No way," Quint said emphatically. "The only reason I know about this stuff is that one of the hands on the Three Pine Ranch got married."

"Did the marriage last?"

"Three years and going strong, last I heard. That's a year longer than the boss's daughter, who got married with all the usual hoopla that kept the whole household in an uproar for six months and cost her father a fortune."

"And your point is?"

"That it isn't the kind of ceremony that you have that determines whether a marriage succeeds or not."

Aileen considered this for a moment. "You're undoubtedly right."

"Look, Aileen, I'm pretty sure that going before the justice of the peace isn't the kind of ceremony you've dreamed about. You probably wanted the bridesmaids, the reception, and all the other trimmings that go along with a big shindig. You think we could arrange something like that in a week's time?"

"No. And it isn't necessary. A big wedding is to bring the two families together. Neither one of us has any family."

"True." Quint studied her face for a moment. "What's bothering you?"

"What do you think makes a marriage successful?"

"You're asking me?" Quint looked at her with a raised eyebrow. "I was brought up by a single mom and a series of institutions and foster homes, none of which I'd consider a good model for marriage or family life. I'm hardly an expert."

"But you sound as if you have definite opinions."

"I've thought some on the subject. Haven't you?"

"Some," Aileen admitted. She didn't tell him that her idea of marriage hadn't progressed much beyond being swept off her feet by an exciting man who loved her madly and she him. Did this reveal a streak of immaturity in her? Or was she a romantic at heart? Or was it simply that she hadn't met a man who made her think seriously about marriage? Quint's voice interrupted her silent questions.

"Seems to me that the two people involved have to share the same goals and expectations. Agreed?"

"Agreed."

"We both want the Triangle B to succeed. Right?"

"Right." Aileen nodded to emphasize her agreement.

"To get the ranch back on a sound financial basis, we have to pay off the mortgage and pay the IRS. And we have to do this without taking out a loan or selling any land. You agree?"

"Yes. But put like that, it sounds like an overwhelming goal," Aileen said, valiantly suppressing a sigh.

Quint touched her hand in a reassuring gesture. "We're not doing this all at once. We've got twenty years to pay off the mortgage, so that's a long-term goal. And the IRS we'll take care of in a couple of years. It won't be easy, but we can do it."

"So, shared goals and expectations are the most important factors in a good marriage?"

"They rank right up there. But other things are important too. Getting along. Liking and respecting each other. Being considerate."

"Sounds like you're describing friendship," Aileen said.

Quint's brow drew together in concentration. Then he nodded. "It strikes me that successful marriage partners have to be friends as well."

Quint hadn't said a thing about love. Probably just as well, since the word had no part in their relationship. Still, she couldn't repress the disappointment and sadness that filled her. She had expected so much more when she married.

"You don't look the least bit enthusiastic. What's bothering you?" Quint wanted to know.

She couldn't tell him. She shrugged. "Nothing."

"That won't do, Aileen. We have to be honest. Otherwise we have no chance."

"You're right." She took a deep breath. "What you're saying is true, logical, rational, and, if you throw in a few 'parties of the first part' and 'whereases,' it could be a contract between business partners."

"We *are* business partners," Quint pointed out. "And a marriage license is basically a contract."

Aileen bit her lip in frustration. He still hadn't said anything about the intimate part of marriage. Maybe he wasn't interested. Maybe he was a cold man. No, she couldn't have misread him that badly. The way he looked, that potent masculine aura that surrounded him, unmistakably suggested that he was a passionate man. Maybe she just didn't appeal to him. Or not enough for him to want her as a real wife.

"I said we'll be business partners, but that's not all," Quint said.

"I know. You said you hoped we'd be friends."

"Yes, but that's not all either."

Aileen looked at Quint, waiting. He sat quietly, as if he was mulling over what he wanted to say. This couldn't be good. Aileen steeled herself.

"I like women."

This was worse than she had anticipated. He was about to tell her that he'd have affairs. Aileen clenched her hands into fists. "What are you trying to say, Quint? That from time to time you'll have women on the side the way your father did? But you'll be discreet?"

Quint plunked down his root beer can with a thud. "What? Where do you come off assuming something like this? I told you before—I'm nothing like Jack."

"So you say! But I don't really know you. Why don't you just tell me what you expect."

He took an audible breath to calm himself. "All right. I was going to say that we've already made a commitment to hard work and simple living to save the ranch, remember?"

"Yes. For the next two years."

"Right. So, for those two years we'll share the house as we have in the past. My bedroom downstairs, yours upstairs. We'll be faithful to our vows. No cheating. For either of us. If, after that time, you want out because you've got your eye on someone else, we can talk about it."

Aileen stared at him.

Quint rubbed his chin, feeling suddenly unsure. "Look, I'm giving you an out. If you want it. After our financial situation has improved."

"That goes both ways."

He shrugged. "Yeah, I guess it does. Anyway, two years is a long time. Who knows what can happen in that time?" He smiled at her. "Is there anything else you're wondering about?"

Aileen shook her head. She did wonder what he meant by that, *Who knows what can happen in that time?* statement, but decided not to ask. She didn't think she was up to any more prodigious surprises and changes in her life.

"All right then. I'm going to look at the horses. One of the mares seems to be off her feed."

As soon as Quint was out the door, Aileen pressed the can of root beer against her hot forehead. They were getting married but nothing would change. Well, it hadn't been bad. They didn't argue, or hardly ever. They did want the same things for the ranch. So why did she feel so confused, so uncertain, so sad?

Quint paused on the back porch and let out a deep sigh of relief. He'd gotten Aileen to agree to marry him. Had convinced her that marriage was the best way to save the ranch. It *was* the best way. It was the only way.

Even though she had eventually agreed, she was as nervous and skittish as a mare facing her first saddle. He'd have to proceed very carefully, very slowly, woo her without her noticing—or risk spooking her. That he'd been attracted to her from the very beginning, he'd been aware of. That he liked her better than any woman he'd ever met, he'd discovered driving home when the idea of marrying her had hit him. Maybe liking was too tame a word for what he was feeling. Maybe . . .

Whoa, cowboy. Don't get ahead of yourself. One thing at a time. And time was on his side. Quint cast one last look at the kitchen window before he took the porch steps two at a time. Whistling some half-forgotten song about sunshine and love, he headed for the barn.

Aileen studied the ring on her finger. She twisted it, admiring the bright, golden sheen of the band that branded her a married woman.

"What's the matter? Doesn't it fit?" Quint asked, pulling out of the courthouse parking lot.

"No, it fits just fine."

"Don't you like it? You said you wanted a plain gold band."

"I like it. It's just right: not too wide and not too narrow. Only it feels strange because I'm not used to wearing a ring. That's all."

She looked at his left hand where she had placed a golden band during the ceremony. Quint had told her that on workdays he wouldn't be wearing the ring. A man he knew got his caught on a wire and nearly lost the finger. It sounded plausible, but Aileen knew she would look at his hand to check for the band whenever they went somewhere together. She frowned. Since when had she become so distrusting? So possessive?

She picked up the small bouquet of delicate pink rosebuds and baby's breath that Quint had ordered for her. She had been deeply touched by the gesture. Not only that, but the flowers had added a small, magical touch to the brief ceremony, had made it more meaningful, and had made her feel more like a real bride. Or how she imagined a traditional bride would feel.

Aileen wanted to touch her lips where she still felt the imprint of his mouth. Quint had kissed her when the justice of the peace had said he could. She had expected a perfunctory kiss. Instead, Quint had kissed her tenderly, with just a hint of heat that had made her insides quiver. Raising the bouquet, she inhaled the exquisite scent of the roses.

"Are you sure you won't change your mind and go out to dinner? I could make reservations somewhere nice. You don't have to cook on your wedding day," Quint said.

"Thanks, but I'd rather eat at home." Aileen felt Quint's gaze on her, but she looked straight ahead through the windshield. She would rather he didn't know how nervous she really was. At home, in her own kitchen, she might manage to eat without spilling food on her new, powder-blue silk dress.

"Quint, I just thought of something. Please pull into the service station up ahead." Aileen consulted her watch and nodded, pleased.

He glanced at her but did as she asked. "You sound excited. What did you think of?"

"I want to invite a few people to dinner. You know, make it a small celebration. Do you mind?" She watched his face carefully to gauge his true feelings.

"That's a great idea. Who do you want to ask?"

"Martha and Bob, of course. And Dora. They're the closest thing to a family I have. And my friend Jennifer and her husband. Is there anyone you want to invite?"

"My buddies are either on the rodeo circuit or in the western part of the state. Your guest list sounds okay to me."

"I don't know why I didn't think of this sooner," Aileen said, shaking her head. Actually, she did know why. All week she had been terrified that the school board would send for her and fire her. She had never been dismissed from any of the jobs she'd held, and the idea of getting fired was both scary and humiliating.

Then she had worried and second-guessed her decision to marry Quint until restful sleep had been impossible.

When it had finally been time to leave for the courthouse, Aileen had been apprehensive as well as relieved. She had never thought that she'd approach her wedding day with a let's-get-this-over-with attitude. Was there ever a bride who'd anticipated her nuptials with such mixed emotions?

Suddenly she remembered the story her mother had told her of the first young wife on the Triangle B. She had been a mail-order bride, arriving in Wyoming Territory from Vermont to marry a man she had never even seen. Aileen glanced at her new husband. She not only knew what he looked like—breathtakingly handsome in a dark gray suit— but she knew his basic character, his plans, hopes, and dreams.

"Here we are," Quint announced.

Here we are? Aileen looked at him again. Quint never stated the obvious. Did that mean he was nervous too? If he was, he hid it well. He opened the door for her and extended his hand to her to help her out of the car. Even though she was no longer unfamiliar with the slightly rough feel of his hand, the touch still sent a small ripple of shivers through her.

In the back of the combination service station and con-venience store, Aileen used the pay phone to make her calls.

Quint filled the tank with gasoline and then joined her.

"Can they come?" he asked

"Everyone except Jennifer's husband. Andy is a truck driver and won't be home till Friday."

"Do we need to buy anything for the dinner?"

Mentally Aileen reviewed the menu she had quickly put together. "Only a bag of charcoal. We have great steaks in the freezer. Let's grill them. It's a lovely day."

"Sounds good to me." Quint picked up a large bag of

briquettes, paid for it, and held the door for Aileen to precede him to the car.

When they were underway again, he asked, "What are you going to tell everyone tonight?"

Aileen looked at him, surprised. "I don't think we need to say anything except that we got married. That's explanation enough."

"Won't they ask questions? This wedding did come out of the blue."

Aileen thought about that for a few seconds. "How about saying that in light of the school board's position, we decided to get married now instead of waiting until August."

"August? Why then?"

"Because it would have taken that long to plan a traditional wedding."

"You think they'll buy that?"

"Why not? They'll think you swept me off my feet and we're crazy about each other."

Taken by surprise, Quint jerked the steering wheel, making the car swerve onto the shoulder of the road. Quickly he brought it under control. "Sorry," he muttered.

In the silence that followed, Aileen studied her bouquet in a seemingly nonchalant manner.

"So, I swept you off your feet," Quint said, his tone musing.

"Why not? It sounds believable. I'm sure you've swept any number of women off their feet."

"But never a woman like you."

Aileen turned to look at him. The hot glint in his eyes took her breath away.

"It's reassuring to know that you think I could sweep you off your feet."

"I didn't say that exactly. I meant that the others will think so."

"You have doubts I can do it? I see I have my work cut out for me. But then I've never shied away from work or from a challenge."

His voice was silky, his grin cheeky, and it occurred to Aileen that unless she put on boots of lead and steel, sweeping her off her feet wouldn't be much work, or much of a challenge for him at all.

Aileen stuck pink candles into the hurricane lamps, replaced the glass cylinders, and stepped back to look at the table.

"Looks nice. Festive," Quint said, entering the screened porch at the back of the house.

"Thanks. It's such a pleasant evening, I thought we'd eat out here." She fluffed the chintz pillows of the wicker chairs that flanked the glass-topped table. "Mom often served dinner on the porch. I loved eating here."

"You miss her," Quint observed.

Aileen nodded.

"Especially today," he added softly. "Of course, if she had lived, the ranch probably would never have gotten into a financial mess, and you wouldn't have had to marry me."

"Or you me. This works both ways," she reminded him.

"True, except I don't view this marriage as quite the disaster you seem to think it is."

Aileen stared at him, struck mute.

Quint reached out and smoothed back a strand of hair that had escaped the Spanish comb holding it off Aileen's face. The touch loosened her tongue.

"I haven't said anything that could lead you to think I view our marriage as a disaster. Where did you come up with that idea?"

"You haven't said so, but your hand trembled when I held it during the ceremony."

Aileen's mouth nearly dropped open. "And that led you to this . . . this strange conclusion? I was nervous! Is that so surprising? I've never gotten married before." She turned toward the door. "Sh. Someone's coming." The crunching sound of footsteps on the gravel walk alerted them that the first of their guests had arrived even before Martha and Bob rounded the corner.

"Hey, there," Martha called out. "I know you said I didn't need to bring anything, but the first of the spinach was ready to be picked. I know how much you like spinach salad."

"That's wonderful! Come on in. I've got some mushrooms in the fridge and walnuts in the pantry. I may skip the steak and eat only salad."

"Speaking of steak," Quint said to Bob, "let's go check the meat." The men went outside.

Although Aileen noticed that Martha kept flicking curious glances at her, she chose to ignore them. No way did she want to answer the storm of questions that their announcement was going to elicit twice. She only hoped that Dora, who was usually the most punctual of women, wouldn't be late today, of all days.

When Martha opened the refrigerator, she did a double take. "You sure have been busy. You even baked a cake. I know it isn't your birthday. Is it Quint's?"

The question stopped Aileen in her tracks. She didn't even know her new husband's birth date. What else didn't she know?

"I just felt like baking a cake," she said quickly. "Would you put the rolls in the oven to get warm, please?"

Martha place the foil-wrapped rolls next to the scalloped

potatoes in the oven. Then she crossed her arms over her chest. "Aileen, what's going on?"

Mercifully, the doorbell rang. "Our other guests have arrived," Aileen said. She hurried out of the kitchen, glad to escape Martha's questions.

Chapter Ten

Aileen greeted her new guests and escorted them to the porch.

"What a lovely bouquet," Dora said. Taking in the candles, the lace tablecloth, and Ruth's good china, she added, "This doesn't look like an ordinary dinner."

"That's what I said," Martha chimed in. "Aileen even baked a cake. Her special coconut cake with the lemon-lime filling. She only bakes that cake for special occasions."

By now all eyes were focused on Aileen. She looked at Quint, who nodded. He came and stood beside her.

"You're both right. This is no ordinary Wednesday night supper," Quint said, and draped his arm over Aileen's shoulders.

The gesture of support heartened her. *Here goes,* she thought, and took a much-needed breath. "Quint and I got married today." The silence that followed her stark announcement was absolute. The only sound she heard was the tumultuous beating of her own heart. Drat. She hadn't meant to blurt the words out quite so bluntly.

The first sound to break the shocked quiet was Jennifer's delighted squeal.

"I knew it! I knew this was going to happen the first time I saw you two together." Jennifer jumped up and hugged Aileen and then Quint.

Aileen couldn't tell who came forward next, for everybody seemed to be hugging and congratulating her and Quint simultaneously. Questions and comments came faster than either could answer them.

"Hold on, folks." Quint finally managed to make himself heard over the voices. "Let me just say that Jennifer was right. Aileen and I . . . we were sort of inevitable. So, we decided to get married right away."

When Quint paused, Aileen said, "Since you're all the family that either of us has, we didn't see the need for a big, traditional wedding. You're here now to help us celebrate."

Martha nodded. "Very sensible. I never could see why people made such a circus out of a simple ceremony."

"I agree with Martha. And it will stop all that nonsense with the school board and save us a lot of unpleasantness," Dora said, her voice approving.

"Great for the ranch," Bob added. "Miss Ruth couldn't have asked for a better man than Quint to run it."

"I couldn't agree with you more." Quint had proven himself to be a good manager. Maybe too good. He had a tendency to go ahead and do things without consulting her. That bothered her. They'd have to come to some sort of compromise.

"We appreciate all your good wishes, but Aileen cooked a wonderful meal—"

"Which is getting cold. Please, everyone, sit down," Aileen said. "You must be hungry by now."

Jennifer punched Aileen playfully on the arm. "You rat. I can't believe you didn't even tell me, your best friend."

"Well, best friend, knowing how you are about keeping a secret, I would have had to tell everyone."

Jennifer started to object, but ended up sheepishly admitting that Aileen was right. "I just get so excited I have to share the news with someone. I can't help myself. Never could. So, what did you wear?"

"A new silk dress. Pale blue. I'll show you our wedding portrait as soon as we get it. Quint hired a photographer."

"Cool," Jennifer said, and flicked Quint a look of approval.

"I want to see it too. Me and Bob got married right after he got back from Korea. He wore his uniform, and I had a beige suit with the prettiest corsage pinned to my shoulder."

"And one of them funny flowerpot hats," Bob added. "Martha, pass the potatoes, please."

"It was a *pillbox* hat," Martha added, with a disdainful look at her husband. She held the bowl of potatoes for a moment as if considering whether Bob ought to have any after the disparaging remark about her hat. Finally she thrust the bowl at him. "It *was not* a funny hat. It was stylish. A few years later Jackie Kennedy made that hat famous."

"Andy and I drove to Vegas on his Harley and got married there," Jennifer said. "We both wore our new black leather outfits. It was so cool." Jennifer sighed, a dreamy expression on her face. Then, her forehead creased thoughtfully, she said, "Isn't it weird that none of us here had a traditional wedding?"

"I'm only sorry about one thing. No champagne. If I'd known, I would have brought a bottle and we could have toasted the newlyweds," Dora said.

"We can still do that. I've got a bottle chilling," Quint said.

"You have?" Aileen asked. Her new husband was full of surprises.

"I hid it behind the milk carton. Do we have wine glasses?"

Aileen liked Quint's use of the word *we*. And that he'd thought to buy the wine. "We not only have wine glasses, we even have champagne flutes. We can do this in style. I think the champagne will go great with the cake."

"The dinner was a hit," Quint said as they were cleaning up the kitchen. "Don't you think so?"

"Yes," she said, with a smile to reassure him. If he needed reassurance. She wasn't that good at reading Quint yet. "Once they got over the shock of our marriage, they enjoyed the dinner." Pausing in the act of hand-drying the fine china plates, she said, "Actually, they took it better than I thought they would. It was almost like they were thinking, 'We're surprised, and yet we aren't really, because we expected it.' What an odd reaction. And they all had it, even Dora. I thought she might have a few reservations."

"Aren't you glad that they approved?"

"Of course. It'll make life easier." Deep down, had she expected to have to defend herself to Dora? To list all the reasons why it had been necessary to get married to Quint? If so, why? Maybe to reassure herself yet again? Possibly.

Aileen stole a look at Quint. He didn't seem to be plagued by doubts and second thoughts. His hands were steady while hers were a little shaky. Not a good thing when handling her mother's good china.

"Where do these dishes go?" Quint asked.

"In the china cabinet in the dining room. If you'll set

them on the dining room table, I'll put them away tomorrow."

"You trust me with them?"

*Why not, since I'm trusting you with my life, my future,
and my heart.* Aloud she said, "You seem to have steady
hands." She watched him carry the tray of plates out. Then
she looked around the kitchen. Everything was put away.
Now what?

Should she say good night and go up to her room? Pretend this was just like any other evening they'd spent together and not her wedding night? If only she had more
experience with men, if only. . . . Quint returned, cutting
short her fruitless dithering.

"Looks like we're all done in here," he said.

Aileen nodded. She folded the dishtowel and then shook
it out and refolded it again. Before she could repeat the
process, Quint was by her side. He took the dishtowel from
her hand and laid it on the counter.

"You're nervous," Quint said with a frown. "You were
not nervous around me before, not even that first night
when I was a total stranger and barged in on you, bold as
brass, and demanded a room in your house."

Aileen shrugged, careful not to meet his eyes. "You were
only my partner in the ranch then. Nothing else."

"And now I'm your husband, and that makes you nervous?"

"Why wouldn't it? It adds a whole new dimension to our
relationship."

Quint shook his head, a little bewildered. "Women sure
are complicated. Correction, some women are."

"Meaning me?"

"Meaning you."

"Why? Because I'm not sure that getting married was
the right thing to do?" Quickly Aileen shook her head.

"What am I saying? It *was* the right thing to do. Of course, it was. We had no choice."

"But you wish we'd had a choice?" Quint asked softly.

"Sure. Don't you?"

"Let me ask you something. Do you think that you and I could have shared this house forever, with you upstairs and me downstairs, without anything happening between us?"

Aileen didn't know what to say. When she remembered all the dreams she'd had about Quint, she felt blood rush to her face.

"We're attracted to each other. If you deny that, you're lying to yourself."

When she didn't say anything, but looked at him with wide, wondering eyes that he thought held a trace of panic, he added, "Oh heck, Aileen. What I mean is, I'm not going to drag you by your beautiful hair to the nearest bed, so relax. I like my women warm, willing, and showing some initiative."

"Oh."

"Well, it's been a long, full day. I'm turning in." Quint bent down and placed a kiss on her forehead.

Aileen watched her husband walk out of the room. On her wedding night. With just a kiss on her forehead. Once again her feelings were all over the map, ranging from relief to disappointment to worry. Quint's words, *showing some initiative*, scared the living daylights out of her. What exactly did that mean?

Here she was, a well-read, educated woman, who was abysmally ignorant about male-female relationships. It wasn't that she didn't know about procreation, but knowing the biological facts didn't help one bit when she faced Quint. When she looked into those mesmerizing green eyes of his, she understood why women swooned. At least those in novels did. Or used to. In the nineteenth century.

Get a grip. Swooning hardly qualified as showing initiative. It probably hadn't even occurred to Quint that she lacked experience.

Aileen massaged her temples. Maybe reading or rereading some of the great love stories would give her a clue about this man-woman conundrum. But not the *Anna Karenina* or *Madame Bovary* kind of novels. Those ended tragically. What she needed were modern love stories, featuring heroines who knew about initiative. When she realized she was thinking of consulting books, she rolled her eyes. She was taking the intellectual approach. Or, as Quint would say, she was being "teachery."

When she got home from school the next day, Quint joined her immediately. He must have been waiting for her.

"So, how did it go? Anybody give you a hard time?" he asked, while pouring her a cup of coffee.

"It went more smoothly than I'd hoped."

"That's good." He handed her the coffee.

Aileen sat down and with a sigh slipped her feet out of her pumps. She inhaled the aroma. "You must have just brewed this. I sure can use it. Thank you."

"You're welcome." Quint poured himself a cup and sat down at the table across from Aileen. "Tell me what happened."

"I went to the office to check my mailbox. The sub had left me notes, as I'd asked. I'll have you know that my kids behaved reasonably well, which is good, since I'd threatened them with a week's worth of lunch detentions or the loss of a big toe, whichever they preferred."

Quint grinned. "You're a toughie, aren't you? I bet the kids like that even if they pretend they don't."

"I don't know about that," Aileen said. "Anyway, there were a few people in the office, which was perfect. Too many and my announcement might have been lost in the noise, and too few, they'd have asked questions. I was just steeling myself to speak when the principal came in. This was ideal. So I said to the secretary that she might want to change the name on my box, as it was now Fernandez. I told her I was sorry that my married name would mess up the alphabetical arrangement of the boxes. I handed her my signed absence form and left."

"What was the reaction?"

"Stunned silence while I was there. What was said later?" She lifted her shoulders in a shrug. "Anyway, in my classroom I wrote 'Mrs. Fernandez' on the board. Though they all read it, none of my homeroom students asked about it until Norman arrived. In my mind I think of him as Norman the Nosy. Predictably, he asked if Mrs. Fernandez was another sub. I told him that it was my new name. He said congratulations and in the next breath asked if he could go to his locker. After correcting his 'can I go' to 'may I go' once again, I told him he could." Aileen stopped to take a sip of coffee.

"Go on," Quint said.

"I took attendance and reminded the kids to pay attention to the announcements which had come on over the PA. After the baseball team was congratulated on its victory, Norman's voice came on loud and clear, announcing that I was now Mrs. Fernandez. He congratulated me and invited the students to come by my room to wish me well. At first I wasn't sure whether I should be annoyed with Norman, but then I realized he saved me from having to tell umpteen people individually."

"I like Nosy Norman," Quint said with a grin.

"Actually, I do too."

"How did the rest of the day go?"

"Okay, except for a couple of snide remarks about getting married just to keep my job, which I tried to ignore." She paused for a moment. "You know, if this marriage doesn't work out, I'll get an awful lot of snide remarks."

"Why wouldn't it work out? We have too much at stake for it not to work out," Quint said, his voice rock steady.

Work.

That seemed to be the operative word for the next month. With school drawing to a close, there were a lot of after-school activities Aileen had to attend. There were finals to give, grades to hand in, textbooks to count and store, and her desk to empty. At home she spent the remaining daylight hours in the garden. She had never put in such a big garden single-handedly. When graduation ceremonies were finally over, she heaved a sigh of relief. Now she could concentrate on her work at home.

During the week between the end of the semester and the beginning of summer school, Aileen washed all the windows and the curtains. She cleaned out closets and drawers. She waxed all the floors. She worked feverishly— in part to get the work done, in part to deal with her disappointment.

Quint hadn't come to the graduation ceremony, though he had promised. She'd had to put up with a number of less-than-tactful comments about the conspicuous absence of her new husband. But what made her even more angry was the fact that he hadn't spent any time with her. Aileen knew how much work there was on the ranch, knew he barely took time out to eat and sleep, but still, his total neglect of her hurt.

By Friday there wasn't a corner of the house she hadn't scrubbed, shined, or straightened out.

Unexpectedly, that morning, Quint joined her in the kitchen. As he poured himself a cup of coffee, he looked around. "Everything in the house sparkles. Any special reason for your cleaning frenzy?"

"Cleaning frenzy? Is that what it looked like to you?"

"Yes. I've never seen anyone clean like that."

Aileen shrugged. "Just spring cleaning. I usually do it just before summer school."

Quint frowned. "I thought you said you were done going to summer school?"

"I am. I'm talking about teaching summer school."

"Oh? You haven't mentioned teaching summer school."

Quint had crossed his arms across his chest. His green eyes were cool, guarded. Patiently she said, "I didn't mention it because I only received the call on Wednesday telling me I got the summer school assignment."

"That was two days ago."

His accusatory attitude annoyed Aileen. "I can count. I know it was two days ago."

"You didn't think it was important to tell your husband that you're planning to teach summer school? That this wouldn't affect me?"

"Don't worry. You'll get your meals on time."

"I'm not worried about my meals. I managed to get myself fed for quite a few years without your help. What I am worried about is your failure to tell me what you're doing. You act as if you lived in this house alone."

Aileen gulped before her voice could squeak past the anger that tightened her throat. "I act as if I lived in this house alone? When am I supposed to tell you anything? You're hardly in the house long enough to gobble down your food. Am I supposed to chase you down on the range? That is if I could even find you, since you don't bother to tell me what section you're working. You act as if the ranch belonged only to you!"

Quint's eyes narrowed. "I'm aware that I only own half the ranch. You don't need to remind me of that."

Aileen ignored his comment. "But even if I'd told you about summer school, you probably wouldn't have heard me."

"When haven't I listened to you?" he demanded.

"I invited you to attend the graduation ceremony with me. It was last Sunday afternoon. You said you would come. You didn't. I thought you could spare a couple of hours. Obviously I was wrong. Everything else is more important."

Quint smacked his forehead. "Aileen, I forgot. One of the tractors broke down and I just forgot. I am sorry."

"Sometimes sorry isn't enough."

"I know that, but you're wrong about everything else being more important."

"Really? You could have fooled me."

"Being sarcastic isn't going to help anything."

"Wrong. It helps me feel a little better." She walked towards the door.

"Where are you going?"

"To pull some weeds before they take over the garden." And vent her anger. Looking at him, she asked, "Is there anything else?"

"Don't be so darned polite. It drives me up the wall."

"I'm glad something makes you notice me, even it it's in a negative way."

"Oh, I notice you, believe me," Quint said.

"Really?"

"Really. Now, spit it out."

"Spit what out?"

"Whatever is making you so hopping mad at me. I didn't

realize it before, but you are nail-spitting furious with me."
Quint shoved his hands in the back pockets of his jeans.
He waited, his temper carefully leashed.

"Really?"

"Aileen, nobody can invest more ladylike sarcasm in the
word 'really' than you can. I told you I was sorry I forgot
about the graduation ceremony." His eyes narrowed. "But
I've a hunch this is about something else. What? And if
you say 'really' again, I swear I'll let loose with a streak
of words that'll blister your schoolmarm ears."

"All right, you asked for it. We've been married for a
month, and in these four weeks we've been together less
than in any one week before then. What kind of life is
that?"

"There's just so much darn work that needs to be done
right now," he said. That was true, but it was also easier
to be out on the range than in the house near her where he
could be tempted to grab her and kiss her senseless. All
these weeks he'd been waiting for some sign from Aileen
that she was ready to be his wife, but so far she'd remained
as unapproachable as ever. In the meantime, he'd worked
as hard as he could to prove himself to her. "There's a lot
of work," he repeated.

Aileen tossed her hair. "Tell me something I don't know.
But the work isn't going to slow down until November, if
then. So, in the meantime, what do we do? Nod to each
other as we pass in the hall? Grunt a good morning—"

"No, we don't. You want to live like that?"

"If I did, I wouldn't have brought up the subject."

This could be the sign he'd been waiting for. Quint was
sure his palms were sweating. He felt his heart pound in
his chest. Very casually he said, "We need to take some
time off from work."

A voice outside called Quint's name. "The hands are

waiting for me, but we'll go to a movie or do something else this weekend." When she didn't respond, Quint said, "Aileen, I'm asking you for a date."

Somewhat taken aback, she asked, "Really?"

"It may be a little unusual for a man to ask his wife for a date, but that's what I'm doing. How about going to a movie tomorrow night?"

"I'll look in the paper to see what's playing," she said, trying not to sound overly eager.

Quint smiled at her over his shoulder before he left.

Aileen hummed and executed a little dance step. When she realized what she was doing, she stopped. They were only going to a movie. That was no reason to be so happy. Yet she was.

She sighed. All it took was a smile from Quint and a promise to spend time with her, and she was willing to forget all her grievances. Worse, she was willing to overlook that Quint had already forgotten his promise to keep her up to date on what he was doing.

Aileen shook her head, bemused. Is this what happened to women when they were strongly attracted to a man? They turned into pathetic creatures who grew weak at the sight of their man?

Chapter Eleven

"**Y**ou're sure there's nothing playing you'd like to see?" Quint asked as they cleaned up the kitchen after dinner.

"I'm positive. The choice is between one of those sickeningly sweet animated films and a slasher movie."

Quint grimaced. "I could sit through the animated movie if I were taking our children, but not otherwise."

Our children. Aileen's heart skipped a beat. They had not discussed having children. But then they hadn't discussed much of anything recently.

"What else is there to do? I'm trying to picture the buildings along Main Street. Wasn't there a pool hall a little south of Ruby's Cafe?"

Aileen nodded. "If you want to play pool, we don't have to go all the way into town. There's a pool table downstairs."

"Oh yeah? You play?"

"No. Jack thought that pool was strictly a man's game."

"Not very open-minded of Jack," Quint remarked.

150

"He had fairly immovable opinions on many subjects. Want to go downstairs and take a look?"

"Sure. Lead the way."

Aileen did. When she turned on the lights, Quint whistled.

"This is some game room," he said, looking around.

Aileen touched the bar. She looked at her hand and shook her head. "I don't get down here as often as I should." She grabbed a bar towel and started polishing the lovely wood.

"Stop that," Quint said. "You've cleaned enough."

"It is a good-looking bar, isn't it? I remember Mom saying that they got it from an old saloon and had it refinished. The wood's mahogany and the rail is brass. If we ever get desperate for cash, we could probably sell it for a nice chunk of change. The pool table too, though I'm no expert on its quality."

Quint examined the table. "It's solid and well-made. Definitely not cheap." He examined the cue sticks in the rack on the wall. When he saw the long, narrow case, he whistled again. "Jack's?" he asked.

Aileen nodded. "He never let anyone touch it, or his sticks."

"He must have been a serious pool player." Quint ran his finger over the finely-grained leather case.

"He was. He used to invite a bunch of men. They'd smoke cigars, sip bourbon, and play."

Touching the initials on the case, Quint asked, "Who's MJB?"

"Martin Jack Bolton. Jack's father. Your grandfather," she added softly. He looked startled. And, for a moment, pleased. Then his green eyes studied the cue stick with far greater interest than it merited.

"Know anything about him?" he asked, his tone casual.

"Not really. When I asked about him, Jack's face assumed that stony expression that clearly cut off all discussion. Now I wish I'd pressed him to elaborate. I'm sorry, Quint."

"You have nothing to be sorry about." Quint tested one of Jack's cue sticks.

"Where did you learn to play?" she asked.

"At the Duggans. One of the foster homes I stayed in."

"How old were you at the time?"

"Thirteen, going on fourteen."

"Wasn't that a little young to teach someone how to shoot pool?"

Quint shrugged. "Mr. Duggan thought I was old enough. And that I was a natural." Quint paused for a moment. "Looking back, I realize that he was a hustler. Know what that is?"

Aileen nodded.

"He taught me to play over the loud objections of his wife. She maintained that pool was the devil's game. Worse, it was gambling, one of the cardinal sins in her opinion." Quint grinned. "Never mind that she played bingo twice a week. I guess if you did it at the parish hall, it wasn't gambling."

"You sound as if you liked the Duggans."

"They were okay."

"How long did you stay with them?"

"A little over a year. She got sick, so the child care people split the kids up and placed us in other foster homes. I've often wondered what happened to the others."

Aileen kept quiet, not wanting to break into his reminiscences. Quint was sharing his past with her, something he had never done before unless she questioned him.

"Even after I left the Duggans', I didn't stop playing

pool. I played as often as I had the chance and the money, and the pool hall owner didn't chase me out because I was too young."

"I suspect you were a little pool shark."

Quint grinned. "How'd you guess? But only until I was old enough to hold down a job and earn money legitimately."

"But you didn't stop playing then either?"

"No. I enjoy the game. And it's a good way to pass the time and keep from having to drink too much. You can nurse a bottle of beer through several games."

"You don't like to drink?"

"Not particularly. It slows down your reaction and your performance. When you're rodeoing, that's bad." Quint paused for a moment. With a suggestive grin, he added, "Drinking also slows down your performance in other activities. Activities I like even more than rodeoing."

When Aileen understood the implications of his statement, she felt warmth creep into her cheeks. To distract him, she turned on the radio. "Would you like a soft drink?"

"Not right now. Thanks. Why don't you come over here? I'll teach you to shoot pool."

"No, thanks. I don't think I'd be very good at it."

"You don't know that till you try. Come on, Aileen."

That soft, coaxing voice drew her like a magnet, even though she was sure she didn't want to learn to play pool. She stopped a couple of feet away from him and watched him test several cue sticks. He handed her one.

"This is how you hold it," Quint instructed, standing behind her and reaching around her with both arms to adjust the cue.

He was so close that his body pressed lightly against hers. She felt his breath feather against her temple. She recognized the pine scent of his soap and wondered how a simple soap could smell so good.

"Relax your grip, Aileen."

She tried, but her fingers seemed to be glued to the stick.

"You smell sweet, like caramel."

"You like caramel? I saw a recipe for caramel custard recently. Maybe I'll try fixing it one day."

"I do like caramel," he murmured. "Love the way it smells." And fate had given him a wife who smelled like that. He couldn't stop himself from pulling her closer.

"You're so tense," Quint murmured. "Relax."

Relax? How could she relax when his nearness made her knees shake? She had longed to be with Quint, but to talk, to get to know him, not to have her senses reel and her body grow weak. Aileen let go of the cue and ducked under Quint's arm. Quickly she moved several feet away.

"I don't think I can learn to play pool."

"Why not? It's not that hard."

"I'm not good at playing games."

"You also said you weren't good at dancing, and look at you now. Your moves take my breath away." Quint took her arm and pulled her against him again. "Turn around," he ordered. When she did, he placed her hand on the cue stick and his hand on hers.

Once again Aileen found herself imprisoned in his arms.

"You have a lot of undiscovered talents and abilities," he murmured.

"You think so?" Aileen's voice sounded throaty. She couldn't seem to breathe properly.

"The way you respond to music convinces me you'd respond as intensely with your other senses. You don't believe me?"

Aileen shrugged.

"Let's try an experiment." Quint took the cue stick from her hand and turned her to face him.

Aileen tried to put a little distance between them, but he had her trapped against the pool table.

"Close your eyes," Quint instructed.

"Why?"

"It's part of the experiment. Trust me." Seeing the wariness on her face, he realized that she probably wasn't comfortable with or used to being touched by men. She'd admitted to not having dated much in the past year or so, and Jack, he guessed, hadn't been a toucher. Gently he said, "I won't hurt you. I'd never hurt you."

She looked searchingly into his eyes. Then she nodded.

"Touch my face," he said softly. When she hesitated, he raised her hand to his cheek. "What do you feel?"

"Your skin. It's warm. Your beard's a little prickly, but, oddly enough, it's sort of a pleasing sensation," she added, surprised.

"Touch my hair."

Aileen had been wanting to do just that since she couldn't remember when. At first she touched his hair only with her fingertips. Then, boldly, she buried both hands in the black mane. His hair was thick and coarsely silken. "This feels good," she murmured.

Did it ever. Her caressing hands made Quint shiver.

"Time to test another sense," he whispered.

"Which one?"

"Taste. Kiss me."

Aileen's eyes snapped open. "Pardon?"

"You heard me."

"Um. Yes. Taste. I made a dessert. Why don't we taste it?" Nimbly she ducked out of his arms and hurried upstairs.

Quint stared after her in stunned disbelief. Then he

grinned. What she needed was a different approach and a little more wooing. He could do that.

Upstairs Aileen soaked a paper towel in cold water and pressed it against her hot face. She couldn't believe she'd bolted upstairs like a coward. Except his sweetly whispered command to kiss him had caught her completely off guard. None of the men she'd dated had ever asked her to kiss them. They'd just grabbed her and pressed their lips against hers with varying degrees of expertise. Some of those kisses had been more pleasant than others. Quint's kisses, she suspected, would be quite awesome, if merely thinking about them made her heart pound.

She heard Quint enter the kitchen. Moments later music floated from the radio.

"The dessert can wait," he said. "How about a dance? Jennifer mentioned going to The Black Hat. They do mostly line dancing there."

"I don't know how to do that kind of dancing."

Her tone of voice told him that she'd pounced on that as an excuse. "Line dancing isn't hard. And it's okay if you don't do it perfectly."

Aileen looked at him with a raised eyebrow. "Why do you feel it necessary to give me permission not to do something perfectly?"

"Because you won't give it to yourself." When she continued to look at him, he added, "Why do you think you're not into doing something on the spur of the moment?"

"Because I'm conservative by nature?"

"Maybe, but Jack's insistence on being perfect sure didn't help."

"No, it didn't," she admitted, astonished by this insight. "But I'm also not a risk taker."

"Yeah, right! You take risks every day. How do you know that you're getting through to those kids? You don't, but you spend all that energy and time on them. Maybe years down the road one or two of them will come back and tell you that you had a big influence on their lives, but right now? You're gambling and taking risks."

"I hadn't thought of it that way," Aileen admitted.

"And then you live on a ranch. If ranching in this day and age isn't taking risks, I don't know what is."

"You're right."

"Okay then. Come on." Quint held his hand out to her.

"What, right now? We're line dancing in this kitchen?"

"Why not? It's big enough. We have plenty of room."

"Remember, dancing doesn't come naturally to me the way it comes to you."

"Hush. You'll be okay."

"So, what steps are you going to teach me?"

"Depends on what music's playing." Quint didn't let go of her hand while they waited for the commercial to end. "Did you know there are actually teachers out there who teach the steps without music? How can you dance without music? That's ripping the soul out of dancing." He shook his head. "Ah. Listen. A country-western cha-cha."

"You're kidding, right?"

Quint grinned. "No. There really is such a thing as a cowboy cha-cha. It goes like this."

Quint demonstrated, his thumbs hooked in the belt loops of his jeans. Aileen watched. He made it seem effortless. Graceful. Even sexy. Very sexy. This wasn't going to be easy. Thank heaven, he wasn't going to touch her. Still, even being close to him was enough to fluster her and impair her concentration.

"It's easy," Quint said. "You can do it."

Aileen looked at Quint, doubting that line dancing would be that simple. But his warm smile went a long way toward easing her reservations, if not her nervousness.

"Give me your hand," Quint said firmly.

"Why?" she asked, alarmed. "I thought that in line dancing you didn't touch."

"You don't, except when you're learning."

"Oh." Aileen held out her hand. She wondered if he noticed that it trembled, but she didn't look at it or at him.

His large hand enfolded hers. He pressed it reassuringly. They repeated the sequence several times before Quint added the pivots and the quarter turns. The song ended.

"There. Was that so bad?" he asked.

"No, because you're a good teacher."

"Of course I am. Didn't I tell you I'm good at a lot of things?" His cocky tone matched his cocky grin. "Just out of curiosity, what makes me a good teacher?"

"You're patient, you reinforce what you've taught, and you're generous with praise."

"Well, thank you, ma'am." He glanced at their joined hands. "Before? When I said I had to hold your hand to teach line dancing, I lied. It was just an excuse."

It was on the tip of Aileen's tongue to say that he didn't need an excuse since he was her husband, but she stopped herself. Instead, she said, "You cowboys are a sneaky bunch."

"We have to be, or we'd never get to hold hands. What with spending our days with cattle and horses—"

"I get the picture. Any more line dancing tonight?"

"Depends on the music. If this announcer ever stops jawing—"

"He heard you," Aileen said, when the music started.

"Yeah, and he's playing a nice, slow two-step." Quint put his arms around Aileen and drew her close. "I have a confession to make."

"Oh no! Not another one. Are you going to confess you like holding hands . . . um . . . hooves—"

"No, smartie. I'm confessing that I'm not all that crazy about line dancing."

"Really? I wouldn't have guessed that. Why not?"

"No touching. Dancing without holding your partner goes against the spirit of dancing." He frowned. "There's probably a word for what I mean."

"Contrary. Or, if you want to be pedantic, dancing without touching 'contravenes the essence of dancing.' "

Quint grinned. "You're so good with words."

"And you're so good with moves."

"Yeah? And you haven't seen anywhere near all of my moves yet," he murmured against her hair, his voice husky.

The promise inherent in those words caused a shiver of anticipation to shimmy down Aileen's spine.

Quint's arms tightened around Aileen. He felt her back go rigid. "It's okay. Just relax." He moved his hand slowly, soothingly along her spine.

Suddenly, his thoughts wandered dangerously. Would she allow herself to wear lingerie with bits of lace and satin to make up for the modest clothes, or would her underthings be plain and functional as well? But even wearing unadorned cotton lingerie Aileen would be woman enough to make him incredibly happy he was a man. He had no doubts about that.

The song ended, plunging Quint back into reality. He held her a few seconds longer, willing his body to relax, his pulse to return to normal. If that was possible with Aileen still in his arms. He would have to let her go. Reluctantly he did so when the radio announcer's voice slid into an advertising spiel.

"It's getting late," Aileen said quietly.

"Tired?" Quint asked.

She shrugged. "Not particularly, but you get up early,

even on Saturdays. And I plan to spend the day attacking those pesky weeds that are threatening my plants."

"If you don't watch those weeds closely all the time, they'll take over," Quint warned jokingly.

"I've noticed that," she said with a smile. Aileen turned off the kitchen light. Side by side they walked toward the stairs.

Though Quint slowed their pace, they quickly reached the foot of the stairs—his nightly battleground between desire and decency. Every night he was tempted to make a move on Aileen, but hadn't he promised her that he wouldn't drag her to the nearest bed? His bed, he estimated once again, was a scant and scary fifteen feet from where they stood. Way too close.

Aileen raised her face to look at him. He steeled himself against the pull of blue eyes and red-gold hair, the scent of spring flowers and sweet caramel, the taste of soft lips and sweet kisses which were relatively unpracticed and thus triply dangerous and seductive.

"I had fun," she said with a smile. "Good night." Quickly, she ran up the stairs.

At school Aileen stared happily out the window. All she saw was the parking lot, half-empty during the summer session. Or rather, she didn't really see it. What she saw instead, in her mind's eye, was Quint smiling at her. Quint telling her about his day. Quint looking at her with a teasing grin in those green eyes.

A sneeze in the classroom plunged her back into reality. Embarrassed, she glanced at the sixteen incoming freshmen who had signed up for her study skills class. Their heads were bent over their work. Thank heaven, they hadn't seen their teacher's smile, which doubtlessly had been dreamy, if not downright fatuous.

Time to get back to work. Aileen rose from her chair. "Class, as I told you, taking notes does not mean copying word for word. What did I say I would do if I saw a single complete sentence on your index card?"

She glanced at her seating chart before calling on the boy in the second row who had raised his hand. "Yes, Jason?"

"You said you were the card cop and you'd tear up any note card that had a stolen sentence on it."

"That's correct. Thank you, Jason." Aileen walked around the classroom. She stopped to look at the cards of a girl chewing gum vigorously. "Brittany, what is the exception to copying word for word?"

"Putting quotation marks around the sentence," Brittany said and popped her gum.

"That's right. What else do you have to do?"

"Write down the book and the page you got it from."

"Correct. Now get rid of your gum, Brittany. In the trash can, please."

"Aw, Mrs. Fernandez—"

"Now, Brittany. I loathe finding gum stuck under a table or on a chair."

Aileen tore up cards from all but five students. The eleven offenders looked unhappy, but it was the fastest way to break them of the habit of copying without properly citing the source.

Aileen stopped at the last desk. She frowned at the card and picked it up. Finally she handed it back to the student. "What does this mean? *Walls & gerfedy?* she asked, intrigued.

The boy squinted at the words. "You know, walls and the stuff written on them."

"Oh. Graffiti." Aileen bit her lower lip to keep from smiling, which would have embarrassed the boy even more. She turned to face the students. "In this class, spelling counts. I take points off for misspelled words, so use your dictionaries."

Glancing at the clock, she said, "Please hand in your work. Since this is Friday, there's no homework. Enjoy the weekend."

The students cheered.

In the hall she ran into Steve. They walked to the parking lot together.

"So, how's married life?" he asked.

"Fine. I can recommend it. You should try it."

"Not me!" he protested. "I'm too young to be tied down. I'm like a busy bee: too many flowers out there that need servicing. Know what I mean?" he asked with a wink.

"Yes, and your simile is trite."

"I bet you'd flunk me if I were in your class."

"I wouldn't doubt it," Aileen said.

"It amazes me how a woman as attractive as you can be so tough."

Aileen stopped walking to look at him with a frown. "What does one thing have to do with the other? Are you saying that only unattractive female teachers should have high expectations and demand quality work?"

Steve ignored her question. "You know what I always expected to happen? You and me becoming an item."

Aileen just shook her head. "I'm parked over there. Have a nice weekend, Steve."

When she approached her car, she stopped, surprised. Quint seemed at ease, leaning against the trunk, and yet she sensed an aura of tension around him. He wore sunglasses and, though she couldn't see his eyes, she was certain they'd assumed the hard glitter of emeralds. "What's wrong? What happened? What are you doing here, Quint?"

"Nothing's wrong. I had to pick up some calf medicine.

Thought I'd stop by to see you. Maybe take my wife to lunch. That is, if you aren't going to lunch with that . . . Steve."

"Why would I go to lunch with him?"

"Maybe because he has the hots for you? Has he made a move on you?" Quint demanded, uncoiling his body, ready to spring into action.

Aileen blinked. She had never seen Quint like this. So . . . belligerent. "Steve hasn't made advances," she said, not entirely sure if that were true or not. "In any event, I can handle Steve. *Puleese,* as the kids say."

Quint seemed to relax a little. Suddenly it hit Aileen: Wasn't Quint acting like a man who was just a tad jealous? *Oh, if only it were so!*

"You want to get some lunch?" he asked.

"Sure," she agreed with a smile. "You know what I haven't had yet this summer? One of those big ice cream sundaes with strawberries and chocolate sauce and nuts on top. Doesn't that sound good on a hot day like today?"

"Darlin', you're a cheap date," Quint drawled.

"I know. Simple tastes and frugal habits. Can't help it." She sighed dramatically.

A car horn honked at them. Steve passing by. Quint placed one arm possessively around Aileen while he raised the other in a casual wave.

Chapter Twelve

In the weeks that followed, Aileen was busy with school, with her garden, and with surreptitiously watching her handsome husband. Watching and waiting for some sign from him that he considered her as more than a partner and friend. But since the incident with Steve and the flash of jealousy, nothing else had happened. Maybe she'd been wrong about Quint being jealous.

Aileen sighed, something she was doing a lot of lately.

She poured the green beans into the bowl of ice water to stop the cooking process. She had blanched them in preparation for freezing them.

"Hey, Aileen, are you in the kitchen?"

"Jennifer? Come on in. I didn't hear your car drive up."

"I'm not surprised. All these fans make a lot of noise."

"You brought the baby. Hi there, sweetie. I'd take you, but my blouse is all damp and sweaty." Aileen patted the baby's cheek.

"It's like a steam bath in here," Jennifer said. "What are you doing?"

"Getting green beans ready for the freezer."

"Isn't that what you did last week too?"

"Well, yes. I staggered the plantings so the vegetables wouldn't all ripen at the same time."

"I can't believe you're doing all this. Not even your mother did this much."

"She did, but she had Martha to help her," Aileen said.

"So where's Martha?"

"Her married daughter is having a rough pregnancy, so Martha flew to Ohio to be with her."

"Tough break," Jennifer said. "Can I help?"

"Thanks, but freezing and canning is an almost daily chore now. I got carried away when I was planting. Want some green beans?"

"No, thanks. I'm perfectly happy buying them from the store, already in a can or a frozen package. Do you have to harvest all of them?"

"I'm letting some of them dry on the plants."

"But don't you have to pick those and shell them?"

"Yes, but not until the fall."

"When school's in session you'll have even less time for housework." Jennifer studied her friend. "Whatever happened to you and Quint going out with us on Saturday nights?"

"We did go."

"Once. I thought you two enjoyed the evening."

"We did. It was fun."

"Then why haven't you joined us again?" Jennifer demanded.

Aileen sighed. "There's just so much work right now. The hay was ready to be mowed, the oats will be ripe next, there are always vegetables that need to be picked or weeds to be pulled. And there's summer school—"

"And you're dead tired. Aileen, watch it or you'll turn into a drudge. You know, one of those ranch women who are faded and worn-out by the time they're forty and look like they're sixty. And all the time their husbands look years younger and develop a roving eye for every young waitress, barmaid, or what have you in the county."

Aileen paused in the act of wiping down the counter. Before she could say anything, Quint entered the kitchen. Dismayed, Aileen wondered how much he'd overheard. She couldn't tell from his expression, which was cordial and polite as he greeted Jennifer and patted the baby's hair.

"Want a glass of iced tea?" Aileen asked Jennifer.

"No, thanks. I gotta be going. I just came by to remind you about the special band that'll be at The Black Hat on Saturday. Hope you guys can come."

Quint held the door open for her and escorted her out.

Aileen braced her hands on the edge of the kitchen sink. Jennifer's words had hit her hard. Was she turning into a drudge? She hadn't ironed, much less starched, the blouse she wore. No wonder it hung damply, limply from her shoulders. And her hair? She'd pulled it into a ponytail when she'd come home from school. But that was hours ago. By now, rebellious strands had escaped the rubber band and drooped around her face. She felt hot, untidy, unattractive. And Quint had seen her like that. Worse, he'd undoubtedly heard Jennifer's words. He would now carry the image of her as a future drudge. Great. Just great.

Quint returned. Aileen busied herself scrubbing the kitchen sink.

"I'm glad Jennifer came by to remind us about Saturday. I hadn't realized how long it's been since we had a night out," Quint said. "Aileen? Is something wrong?"

She shrugged.

He took her by the shoulders and turned her to face him. "It's about what Jennifer said, isn't it? Aileen, you'll never turn into a drudge. You're too intelligent for that. And

you've got the kind of face that'll look good at any age."
He traced her cheekbones. "About Jennifer's other claim?
She's way off base. I won't develop a roving eye."

Aileen couldn't look at him.

"I'm not like Jack."

"I hope not," she murmured. Her adoptive father had
been a cold, reserved man who hadn't seemed to care about
anyone. Well, maybe her mother. A little. Would Quint
ever care about her, really care? Sometimes she thought he
might, and at other times she despaired he ever would. She
just didn't know. And she didn't know how to make him
care.

The blast of a truck horn startled her. "The men are waiting for you."

"They can wait. I have the feeling that something's
wrong. What is it? Do we need to talk?"

She shrugged.

A second and more insistent horn blast tore through the
silence. "You better go," Aileen urged.

She watched him leave, wondering if she should have
taken him up on his offer to stay and talk. No, urging him
to go had been the right decision. She knew how important
the ranch was to him. They had to make it succeed.

Would she ever be that important to him? He was to her.
As much as she loved the Triangle B, she would sacrifice
it for Quint in a heartbeat. Startled, she realized that she
had fallen deeply, irrevocably in love with her husband.

"You know what today was?" Aileen asked Quint, who
looked at her, alarmed.

"Your birthday?"

Aileen dumped a bucketful of tomatoes into the sink to
wash them. "No. That's not until November."

"That's what I thought you'd told me," Quint said, relieved that he hadn't messed up. He couldn't think of any holiday that fell on August first. "I give up. Tell me."

"Last day of summer school."

"Well, hallelujah. You've been working way too hard. You've lost weight, and yesterday I found you sound sleep in that chair over there while you waited for me to come home for dinner."

"Catnaps are good. Lots of people swear by them. And it's been too hot to eat a lot."

"Don't get defensive. I didn't criticize you. How long before regular school starts?"

"Four weeks."

"That's not much time."

She shrugged and concentrated on the tomatoes.

"Why didn't you say something? We could have made plans to go out."

Aileen bit her tongue to keep from snapping at him. They had gone out exactly that one time when Jennifer had practically dragged them to The Black Hat. He had talked about going out again but hadn't done anything about it.

"Haven't you been putting up a lot of tomatoes?" Quint asked, finishing his coffee.

"It's apparently a banner year for tomatoes. Everyone says so."

"Why don't you give some of them away?"

"I have. If I show up with any more at Jennifer's house, she'll lob them at me."

"Okay. Why don't you just leave them on the vine?"

Aileen didn't say anything, but the oblique look she slanted at Quint spoke volumes.

"I better get back to work. Thanks for the coffee." Quint left the kitchen hurriedly.

For an instant Aileen was tempted to pick up a tomato and hurl it after him. All he did was work. All he was interested in was work. Was that all there would ever be? The thought that this might be so nearly broke her heart. Aileen leaned over the sink and cried. She allowed herself to sob until there were no more feelings inside her, until she felt empty and spent.

She splashed her face with cold water. Well, she'd entered into a marriage of convenience, so what did she expect? Rationally, she knew she couldn't expect love, and yet she did. She yearned for it, she hoped for it, she prayed for it.

"Idiot," she muttered. How could she have let herself fall in love with a man who showed no sign that he would reciprocate the feeling?

Aileen gritted her teeth, took two pills for the migraine that had taken hold of her, and finished the huge pot of marinara sauce she had started. She froze all of it except the amount she needed for the pasta dish she fixed for Quint's supper. Then she dragged herself upstairs, slipped into a freshly laundered cotton gown that still smelled of sunshine, and curled into a ball on the bed.

That's how Quint found her, hours later.

"Aileen, are you sick?"

"My head hurts."

"A migraine? You haven't had one in months."

That was true. Not since they'd gotten married.

"Let me massage your temples," Quint offered.

"It's too late for that. I'll just have to ride it out."

"Are you sure? If you sit up—"

"No, no. I need to lie perfectly still. I feel less nauseated that way."

"Can I get you anything?"

"No, thanks. I'm sure I'll feel better in the morning." She felt Quint's hand on her hair, stroking it gently. She thought she felt his lips tenderly touch her hair before he left. Aileen lay still, fighting the nausea, letting the pain wash over her.

She did feel better the next morning when she finally woke up, hours past the time she usually rose. Thinking that Quint had left already, she took a long shower before going downstairs. She came to an abrupt stop in the kitchen doorway.

"Quint, you're still here? Is something wrong?"

He lowered the newspaper he'd been reading. "I wanted to wait to see how you were this morning before I left. How's the migraine?"

"Gone. Knock on wood. Why didn't you wake me? I've made you hours late."

"Aileen, I don't punch a time card."

Except he drove himself as if he did.

"I just made coffee. Want some?" Quint asked.

"Yes."

"Let me get it for you. I don't want you to work so hard. No more canning and freezing. I mean it."

"Just a little more. Until the jars I have are filled. I won't buy any more. I promise."

A knock on the front door startled them. They looked at each other. People they knew came to the back door. "Are you expecting anyone?" Aileen asked.

"No. Are you?"

Aileen shook her head. "I'll see who it is."

She opened the door to a tall, thin woman with graying hair. For an instant she thought there was something familiar about her. "Yes? Can I help you?"

"Are you Aileen Bolton?"

"I'm Aileen Bolton Fernandez."

"I'm Linda Cameron. My maiden name was Bolton."

It took a moment for Aileen to process this information. "Then you're—"

"Jack Bolton's sister. Your adoptive aunt, if there's such a thing."

"Who is it, Aileen?" Quint asked, stepping into the hallway.

Linda's hand flew to her mouth as if to restrain a gasp. As Quint came closer, she dropped her hand. "For a moment I thought you were Jack, the way he looked when he was young," she said, her eyes fastened unwaveringly on Quint.

"Quint, this is Jack's sister, Linda Bolton Cameron. Your aunt."

He managed a polite greeting. "Won't you come in?"

"Yes, please," Aileen added. "There's some fresh coffee."

They made small talk until Aileen had filled their cups and they were sitting around the dining room table.

"You're probably wondering why I'm here," Linda said. "I know Jack passed away this spring. A lawyer from Cheyenne phoned me. I would have come to the funeral, but Dad took a turn for the worse, and I couldn't leave Colorado."

"Is that where Jack is from?" Quint asked.

"Yes. Didn't he ever talk about his family?" Linda asked.

"Not to me. I never met the man," Quint said.

"I know, and I'm real sorry about that. I wish I'd known I had a nephew, but I guess that's water under the bridge, as they say." She turned to Aileen. "Did Jack talk to you about us?"

"No. I knew his father's name, but only because of the initials on the cue case."

Linda chuckled. "Jack stole those sticks from Dad when he lit out. He was fifteen. Couldn't stand living with that mean old man anymore. I got married at sixteen to get away."

"What about your mother?" Aileen asked.

"Ma didn't run away. She died instead. When we were still in grade school." Linda took a sip of coffee. "Ma was a sweet, kind, warm woman. The exact opposite of Dad. He used to beat Jack something awful. I was scared to death of him. Today they'd put him in jail for child abuse." Linda sighed.

"But you're taking care of the old man?" Quint asked.

"Your grandfather. Yeah. So does, did, Jack. That's why I came. To thank you."

Quint and Aileen exchanged a puzzled look.

"Jack put a chunk of money into a bank account to pay for Dad's nursing home. In the will it was mentioned as a bequest, or something like that. I want to thank you for not challenging it."

"It never occurred to us to challenge a bequest," Aileen said, shocked at the very idea.

"I don't know what I would have done if you had. I couldn't begin to pay for his care. I visit him every evening after work. You know, to make sure he eats his supper and takes his medicine."

"I'm surprised Jack left money for his dad's care, given the way he was treated as a child," Quint said.

"Jack said he did it mostly for me. To make my life easier. But, you know, I suspect he also did it for Dad. Blood is thicker than water."

"What's wrong with him? With . . . Granddad?" Quint asked.

"Just old age. He's ninety. Some days he knows who I am and some days he doesn't. That's not unusual for that age." Linda finished her coffee. "Well, I better be on my way."

"But you just got here," Aileen protested. "Why not spend the night and start fresh in the morning? We have a guest room. Or at least stay for a meal."

"It's sweet of you to offer, but I better get back. You know, work and Dad." Linda stood. "Maybe I'll take you up on your offer some other time. Get to know you. Get to know my nephew."

"Yes, I'd like that," Quint said.

They walked Linda to the front door and watched her drive away.

"You have an aunt and a grandfather. A family," Aileen said to Quint. "How does that feel?"

Quint rubbed his neck. "I don't know. I have to get used to the idea of a family."

"I'm glad Linda came and told us about Jack."

"You think his background excuses his behavior?" Quint challenged.

"No, it doesn't excuse it, but it offers some insight into his character. His mother died when he was small, which must have seemed like abandonment to him. And then he was raised by an abusive father who caused him to run away when he was only fifteen. No wonder Jack wasn't a warm, loving man. He didn't know how to be."

"You see the best in everyone, don't you?" Quint stroked her cheek gently.

The way Quint looked at her, his green eyes filled with warmth and an emotion she couldn't identify but liked, made her feel light-headed.

"I better get to work," he said.

Aileen sensed that Quint needed to be alone.

"I'll see you tonight. I may be late," he said and hurried toward the barn.

* * *

The remaining weeks passed much as the whole summer had passed: filled with work. There was much to be said for having work to fill the days. It precluded prolonged fits of brooding.

Not that Aileen didn't still brood in unguarded moments, but her daily schedule didn't allow mammoth indulgences in self-pity, fruitless speculations, and useless longings.

Although Aileen watched Quint—unobtrusively she hoped, and with her fervent love for him well hidden—she saw no change in him toward her. He expressed his appreciation of the meals she cooked for him; he treated her kindly, considerately. And yet she sometimes caught him looking at her, his green eyes watchful, waiting. Waiting for what?

Aileen did see one thing in Quint that was different, one thing that filled her with a flicker of hope. His attitude toward his father seemed to change. For weeks the two photos of Jack she had shown him lay facedown on the desk in the den he used as his office. Then one day when she came to dust, she found them lying faceup in the upper corner of the desk, carefully placed side by side. Quint had looked at them, had to look at them, every time he sat down at the desk.

She put them into a frame which she placed on his desk. Not next to their wedding picture or the photo of him as a boy, holding his mother's hand, but in the same spot where they'd been. When Quint left Jack's photos there, Aileen rejoiced.

If Quint could come to terms with his father's rejection and let go of all those hostile feelings, wouldn't that put a crack into the stone wall he'd erected around his heart? And once that wall was breached, wouldn't he be able to allow himself to feel freely, to trust, to love?

Aileen prayed daily for that miracle to happen; she watched for it, eagle-eyed, but the last week of summer vacation was drawing to an end, and Quint remained silent and distant.

Chapter Thirteen

The next day Aileen decided she had to do something or go crazy. But what? She brooded a long time until she remembered that Quint had said he liked his women to take some initiative. She'd taken the initiative at faculty meetings, in committees, in the classroom. She could take the initiative in her home, couldn't she?

Aileen thought about what she could do, considered strategies, discarded them, formulated new ones. Eventually she came up with a plan. It involved a good meal, a new dress, perfume, and a whole lot of raw nerve and steely resolve.

She put the plan into action the next morning.

Grocery list in hand, Aileen started walking toward her car. Suddenly, she saw the green pickup return to the yard. She opened the car door, but, curious about the visitor, she didn't get in. Early that morning Quint had left with a stranger driving. Now he got out, waved to the driver as he left, and joined Aileen.

"Who was that?" she asked.

176

"Cal McAllister. I met him last week in the feed store. He wanted to look at our north section."

"Why? We don't have any feed planted up there."

"Cal isn't a feed buyer."

Aileen looked at Quint, waiting for him to explain.

"Cal's an engineer." Quint looked at her steadily. "He's a petrochemical engineer."

Aileen reeled as if from a blow to the diaphragm. Blindly she steadied herself against the opened car door. "You had an oil man look at the range? What else did you have him do? A survey? What did you promise? What did you sign?" she asked, afraid of the answer.

"Nothing. Don't get all worked up. I—"

"That's how it starts. They look, then they make you an offer to drill, and then more and more money until you can't say no! How could you do this? I've told you how Mom and I felt about drilling on our land. And once again you didn't even consult me! My Gosh, I was hoping that one day you'd care about me the way I care about you—" Her voice broke.

"Aileen, I—"

She heard Bob call Quint, asking him to look at a foundering horse.

"I'm coming," Quint yelled back.

This was serious, Aileen knew.

"Aileen, the horse could die. I've got to go. We'll talk about this later. I promise." He sprinted toward the stable.

Aileen ran into the house. She was so upset she couldn't even cry. She paced the floor. When the phone rang, she answered it. Anything to distract her.

"I'm so glad you called," Aileen told Dora. "I didn't realize how much I needed to talk to you."

"What's wrong?"

Aileen told her.

Dora was silent for several seconds after Aileen had ended her impassioned outpouring. "You object to drilling for oil on the ranch mostly because your mother did, right?" Dora asked.

"Yes, but I've also seen what the land looks like after the oil company gets through with it."

"That was years ago. They're more environmentally aware now." Sensing Aileen's expression, Dora said, "You're in no frame of mind to listen to logic, so let me just tell you something. Will you listen?"

"Yes."

"When you hang up the phone, look in your illustrated copy of *Alice in Wonderland*."

"Why?" Aileen asked, puzzled but intrigued.

"There's an envelope in there for you from your mother. It's a geological survey of the Triangle B. My copy of the survey is in my safe-deposit box."

Aileen felt the room tilt off center. "Mom had the land surveyed?"

"When she came back from the Mayo Clinic. She knew she wasn't going to get well, so when Jack went on one of his hunting trips, she had the north range surveyed."

"Dad never knew?"

"No. Ruth knew her husband's weaknesses. She was afraid he would start drilling at the first financial setback. She wanted this to be your nest egg, your legacy." Dora paused, letting Aileen take all this in.

"She asked me to keep this a secret until you really needed help. You were still so young when she died. She wanted to protect you. She left it up to my judgment when the right time arrived. I think it has."

There was a long silence on the line.

"Aileen? I wonder if you're really that upset about Quint

letting the engineer look at the north range. Isn't there more
to this crisis than that?" Dora asked.

"Maybe there's more," Aileen admitted softly.

"Such as?"

"Such as my being a fool. I let myself fall in love with
Quint, and he doesn't love me." Aileen stopped, trying to
control a flood of tears.

"Has he said he doesn't love you?"

"No, but neither has he said that he does."

Dora sighed impatiently. "Sometimes I forget how young
you still are."

"What's that supposed to mean?"

"Naturally it's wonderful if the person we love recipro-
cates the feeling. But think of the alternative. Would you
rather *not* love Quint?"

Startled, Aileen drew a sharp breath.

"Think about it, Aileen. If you could, would you like to
stop loving him?"

"No." Her answer surprised her. She tried to imagine not
loving Quint. She couldn't.

"You also have to remember that men don't always, or
even often, express their feelings. Hasn't Quint shown you
in what he does daily that he cares about you?"

Aileen considered that. He had. He did. Small things he
did for her. The way he expressed his appreciation for an
ironed shirt. A pie she'd baked. An unexpected smile, a
brief touch of his hand.

"Well?" Dora demanded.

"Maybe you're right."

"I am always right," Dora said, with a smile in her voice.
"Go look for the survey."

"Do you know what it says?"

"Not exactly, but I have a good idea. Call me later."

Aileen said she would. Then she went in search of the

book. She found the envelope just where Dora said she would. She recognized her mother's handwriting. Tears clouded her eyes. She blinked several times before she could read the words.

For Aileen Bolton, my beloved daughter, to be opened in case of a financial emergency.

Aileen traced the words lovingly.

"Aileen?" Quint came to a sudden stop when he saw her slumped against the hall table. "Are you okay?"

She didn't say anything. She placed the envelope on the hall table with trembling hands.

"Aileen, I didn't hire the engineer. I would never do that without talking to you first. As I said, I met him, we talked, and he asked if he could look at the north section. Apparently that part of the land is nearest to the oil fields north of here." When she remained silent, Quint placed his hand on her shoulder. "Aileen, look at me."

She didn't. She held up the envelope.

"What's that?"

"A geological survey Mom had done before she died. She only told Dora about it."

"Jack never knew?"

"No." Aileen steeled herself to ask, "Do you want out of this marriage so desperately that you want to drill for oil?"

"I don't want out of this marriage. What are you talking about?" he asked, truly perplexed.

"You said that after a couple of years when we're in better shape financially, we might end the marriage. I thought maybe you wanted out earlier, and that's why you were interested in getting the survey done. Even if there were only a small amount of oil, the money would be good."

All Quint could do was stare at Aileen. "Are you bringing this up because you want out?" he asked, his voice hoarse.

She shook her head vigorously.

Quint felt the awful pressure ease from his chest. When Aileen handed him the envelope, he asked, "Have you read it?"

"No."

He tossed the envelope on the hall table.

Aileen looked at him. "Aren't you going to read it?"

"No. I don't want out of this marriage. And I'm not letting you go either."

"You're not?" she asked, barely able to whisper around the lump in her throat.

"Nope. You may as well know that you can't get rid of me that easy." He drew her into his arms for a fierce hug.

He nearly crushed the breath out of her, but Aileen didn't care. She luxuriated in the touch of his strong arms.

"I know I haven't been as attentive as I should have been. I've put work first, but that's because I have to prove myself."

"You don't have to prove yourself to me," she said.

Quint released her. He rubbed his neck.

"Maybe it's me I have to convince that I'm good enough to . . . to own half of this ranch." *And to be your husband.* "Prove that I'm not like my father."

"You're not. You may have inherited half of his DNA, but your character is nothing like his."

"Thanks. Your saying that means a lot. I have to go. The vet's here. He charges by the hour, so I better get back out there and help." Quint walked to the front door. He paused there a moment. "I'll see you tonight."

Aileen stared at the door long after Quint had walked out. Something had shifted between them. She couldn't put her finger on it, but whatever it was, she sensed it was momentous.

Quint was late for dinner. It was just as well, Aileen thought. Given the extra time, she might compose herself. All day she'd been as nervous as the proverbial cat on a hot tin roof.

She had told Quint that she cared for him. He hadn't responded. Maybe he hadn't heard her. Maybe he hadn't wanted to hear this declaration. No, that didn't make any sense. Hadn't he said he wouldn't let her go? He had. And he had hugged her. It hadn't been a friend's comforting hug either. Aileen clung to these two things as if they were a piece of lifesaving driftwood in a storm-tossed sea.

When he came home, she served him dinner, claiming she had already eaten. She didn't think she could keep any food down. She busied herself tidying the kitchen while he ate.

"This was very good. Thank you, Aileen."

"Are you still hungry? Would you like a piece of cake?"

He shook his head. He watched Aileen closely as she put the food away. She had said that she cared for him. What exactly did that mean? He cared for Sweepstake. He cared for the ranch. What he felt for Aileen went way beyond that. Quint didn't know just how he was going to ask her what she meant by caring, but ask her he would. He had hardly been able to think of anything else all day, not even when he'd been helping the vet with the sick horse.

When she hung up the dishtowel to dry, he said, "I'll walk you to the stairs."

It took less than ten seconds to reach the stairs. Both stopped.

"What does it mean, to care for someone?" he asked. He could tell by the pink color tinting her cheeks and by the widening of her eyes that she remembered saying that to him. He watched her struggle for words.

"It means that you're fond of that person. That you have feelings for them." She lifted her shoulders in a small shrug. "I think that's what it usually means."

Happiness flooded through him. Quint wanted to shout like a drunken cowboy. He *was* a drunken cowboy, drunk on joy and rapture. Sensing the tension in Aileen, he controlled his elation. He watched her gaze dart to every corner of the hallway as if looking for a way out. Then he saw her take a deep breath as if she'd reached a decision.

"Remember when you tried to teach me to shoot pool and we talked about the senses?"

"I remember," he said feelingly.

She took another deep breath. "I hadn't planned to do it like this. I mean I wanted to create a romantic atmosphere, but here goes." Aileen placed her arms around his neck. "If you don't mind, I'd like to do that touching thing again."

"I don't mind," Quint managed to say, his voice barely above a whisper. "I don't mind at all." Her touch felt like an electric current burning its way along his nerve ends. If he were a machine, his circuits would have just shorted out and his parts melted down. He felt her eyes look at his mouth. Quint forced himself to stand very still, his arms loosely draped around her waist.

Aileen raised her face to meet his lips. He didn't hesitate, but brushed his mouth over hers in a whisper of a kiss. Her response, though light and unpracticed, was sweet and intoxicating. Encouraged, he wooed her with countless kisses, each one more potent, more urgent. Finally he tore himself away, fearing he might lose control.

"Quint?" she asked softly, tentatively.

"When, if ever, are you going to invite . . . Dammit

Aileen, I'm no saint, so don't go tempting me." Wordlessly he stormed into his room.

Aileen blinked. What on earth had just happened? One moment Quint was kissing her until she nearly fainted, and the next he closed his door and shut her out. She had to find out what had gone wrong.

Resolutely she knocked on his door. Quint opened it almost instantaneously, as if he'd been waiting on the other side. He didn't say anything but looked at her expectantly.

"You said something about an invitation?"

Softly, gravely he said, "In our particular situation it seemed to me that the invitation ought to come from you."

"I'm afraid I'm not familiar with the . . . er . . . etiquette."

"You haven't known a lot of men, is that what you mean?"

"I haven't known any," she whispered.

For an instant Quint was speechless. How could he have been so blind and not sensed this?

"I knew you'd be disappointed. A man like—"

Quint placed his finger across her mouth to stop her outburst. "I'm not disappointed. You caught me off guard, that's all. I'm sorry I've been so dense."

She looked at him, her eyes pleading.

Suddenly he knew what he had to do.

Quint pulled her close. "A woman wants words," he said softly. "You told me that once. Dumb of me not to remember it."

He wrapped his hands in her glorious hair and made Aileen look at him. "Words," he murmured thoughtfully. "I'm not usually at a loss—"

"No, you're not," she agreed.

"But these are hard words to say, even if they're short and simple. Especially that one word. I've only said it to two women: to my mom and to my grandmother, my *abuel-ita*."

Aileen looked at Quint, waiting.

It was now or never. Risk all or play it safe? Since when had safety been that all-fired important to him?

Quint looked at Aileen, looked into those lovely eyes that made him glad he was alive, looked at those lips that kissed him until he trembled like a leaf in a storm. "I'd rather take you upstairs and show you," he murmured.

"Not yet." She realized how hard this was for him. She liked the way he looked at her. She loved him. Why not make this a little easier for him? "I want to ask you some questions first." He nodded. "Do you like me?"

"A lot."

"Do you find me attractive?"

"You make my blood run hot. Aileen, let me cut to the bottom line." Quint took a deep breath. "I love you. I fell for you . . . I'm not sure exactly when, but maybe as long ago as that first time I waltzed you around the kitchen. But we kept telling ourselves that it was better if we kept our feelings businesslike, and that slowed down everything."

Aileen shook her head. "No, it didn't. It gave us a chance to fall in love."

"You said *us*. As you falling in love too? With me?"

"With you. Totally, irrevocably and forever."

"Yeah?" Quint smiled at her. "Irrevocably? I love it when you use fancy words."

"Yeah?"

"Uh huh. Irrevocably, as in not being able to revoke, to take back, to undo?"

"All of the above," Aileen said. "Now what was it you said about taking me upstairs?"